The Return

Even the book morphs!
Flip the pages
and check it out!

Look for other **ANIMORPHS**®
titles by K.A. Applegate:

ANIMORPHS®

The Return

K.A. Applegate

AN
APPLE
PAPERBACK

SCHOLASTIC INC.
New York Toronto London Auckland Sydney
Mexico City New Delhi Hong Kong

The author wishes to thank Lisa Harkrader for
her help in preparing this manuscript.

And for Michael and Jake

Cover illustration by David B. Mattingly
Art Direction/Design by Karen Hudson/Ursula Albano

ISBN 0-439-11522-1

12 11 10 9 8 7 6 5 4 3 2 1   0 1 2 3 4 5/0

Printed in the U.S.A.
First Scholastic printing, December 2000

CHAPTER 1

"On your right is the door to the Oval Office. The office of the President of the United States, perhaps the most powerful person in the world."

Marco threw me a look. One of those looks that said, "If they only knew."

If they only knew there's someone else right here on Earth possibly far more powerful than any president or king or prime minister.

Jake and Marco think it's better people don't know the truth about that someone else.

Me?

Lately I wonder.

Lately I think it might be better to go public.

Let the world know that Earth has been invaded by an alien species led by someone —

something — more evil and more powerful than most humans can probably imagine.

That's what I think.

I'm Rachel.

No last name. You probably already know why. But in case you don't, it's for security. Yours and ours. And it's the same with all of us.

We're the Animorphs. Jake, Tobias, Cassie, Marco, and me.

We're also just kids, at least on the outside. You wouldn't know us if you saw us cruising the mall on a Saturday afternoon or riding a bike down the middle of the street.

Or touring the White House with a bunch of other kids.

Fact: We aren't like other kids.

We were once. But never again.

After a certain point, you just can't go back to where you started. Even if you want to. Which I have to admit — I don't.

To repeat: The Yeerks are here. Parasitic aliens. Their goal is to conquer the human race. And believe me they've been doing it, one human at a time.

But they're getting impatient now. And more aggressive.

Maybe you've seen something about the Yeerks on the Internet.

Maybe also about us. Recently, we were involved in a big throw down on an aircraft carrier out in the middle of the ocean.

And there was an episode with some campers that went bad.

The actual events got some press coverage, but the stories were buried on the back pages. Relegated to Web sites run by sci-fi fans.

The only people who believed the few witnesses with the nerve or dementia to tell the truth about what they saw are pretty much the same folks who believe every nutty story they hear from the media.

Most of the American public thinks the Yeerk invasion story is something straight off the front page of the *Enquirer.* Baby born with antelope snout. Melted Snickers bar in shape of St. Francis's head cures rabies. Yeah, like that's really happening. Or just another urban myth. Like Batman. And alligators in the subway.

I'm not one of those kooks or cranks. And I'm here to tell you that the Yeerk invasion is not a myth, urban or otherwise. The Yeerk invasion is real.

Yeerks are slugs. They crawl into your ear, fit themselves into your brain, and then take control. Which is why hosts are known as Controllers.

The problem with human-Controllers? They

could be anybody. Your sweet mother, your smelly science teacher, the cute pitcher on the local softball team.

And they could be anywhere. At home, at school, at the park.

In the White House.

I glanced at the window. Saw a red-tailed hawk circle in the sky.

Tobias.

One of us. But a *nothlit.* A boy who stayed in red-tailed hawk morph for more than two hours and got trapped there.

Along with Cassie, Tobias is my best friend in the world. Also kind of my boyfriend. The kind with feathers.

It's a long story. But because of an inscrutably powerful being known as the Ellimist, Tobias can morph his human self. Even choose to be that human forever, give up the morphing. The fight. Life as a bird of prey.

But he doesn't choose that option.

Because, just like me, Tobias doesn't want to go back to where he started.

TSEEW!

Faint, but oh, yeah.

Dracon fire!

Half a second later, Tobias crumpled in the air. My heart stopped. The wind sucked out of my

4

lungs. Pain. Disbelief. I watched Tobias plummet to the ground.

A scream. Then lots of screams followed by the sound of crashing doors, splintering wood, breaking windows, and thundering footsteps.

"What's going on?" one of the chaperons shouted.

I already knew. Marco and Jake, too. And Cassie.

The Yeerks were attacking the White House.

Men in slim, dark suits, ear wires tucked into their collars, poured into the hallway. Secret Service. Barking orders.

"Please move quickly toward the exits!"

Two guys herded the crowd toward double doors at each end of the hallway. Jake motioned to us and we stepped out of the flow of panicked people. Gathered around him.

"I can't believe this," Marco hissed. "The White House! You know what this means, don't you? The Yeerks have finally declared war. Open war. No more covert operations."

Yeah. Open war. We'd expected the move, but not in this way. Not an attack on the White House.

Oxygen was returning to my body. And along with it, all the hate I felt for the Yeerks. For what they had done to Tobias. For what they had done to all of us.

I was glad the covert war was over. Glad not to have to pretend anymore.

"Tobias is down," I said. "I saw him get hit. The Yeerks want war, they'll get it."

"Everybody slow down," Jake cautioned. But he looked at me when he said it.

Jake never loses a chance to imply that I'm some kind of shoot-first-ask-questions-later loose cannon.

I gulped some air, tried to slow my pulse. Jake is our leader. We do what he says. At least we have so far. But it gets harder and harder for me. Maybe for all of us.

"Split up," Jake ordered. "Battle morphs. Be ready for action. But don't do anything stupid."

No time to get mad about that "stupid" remark. I knew it was meant for me.

More Secret Service men thundered into the hallway. Broke open the doors to the Oval Office.

I stepped away from Jake and slipped behind a heavy curtain.

I was going grizzly. My biggest, baddest morph.

Just for a moment — just for the goof — imagine a tall, blonde human girl turning into a grizzly bear, in an animated Disney version. No doubt the process would look graceful. Whimsical. Charming, even.

Let me tell you something. The people at Disney do not know squat about the reality of morphing. Not the people at Nickelodeon or the people at DreamWorks, either.

You watch somebody morph, you could lose your lunch.

My face stretched and thickened.

My shoulders bulked up.

I closed my eyes to concentrate, speed the process when . . .

"What's the matter with you? Get out of there!"

I opened my eyes. The curtain had been ripped aside. A Secret Service agent glared at me. I glared back.

"Quit fooling around, kid. We're trying to save your life."

I'd risked my life more times than I could count. Fought every kind of monster the galaxy could muster. And he had the nerve to tell me to stop — fooling around!

Tobias was probably lying dead on the White House lawn.

And this clown wanted me to stop fooling around.

The guy didn't know beans about what was happening on his own watch.

That's when it happened.

Something snapped. Some spring inside me just went BOOINNGGGG!

Maybe when he was lying on the ground in ten pieces he would figure out I hadn't been fooling around.

I wanted blood. I could smell it. I could taste it.

Was it the grizzly in me that wanted to kill?

Or was it the me in me?

I didn't know, and I didn't want to know.

I just wanted to take his face off. I snarled and reached out to slice him from head to toe.

CHAPTER 2

Fortunately for him, I hadn't morphed claws yet. Or teeth. Or much in the way of size.

I caught a glimpse of myself in a mirror across the hall. I didn't look like a grizzly. But I didn't look like Rachel, either.

Bottom line?

I looked like a big girl with a nasty look on her face and a serious hormone imbalance. Long dark hairs sprouted from my chin and cheeks.

"Come on, kid. Quit playing. Get out of here."

The Secret Service guy yanked me from behind the curtain and shoved me toward the exit.

But it was too late.

Two Hork-Bajir-Controllers came crashing into the hallway.

The Secret Service man looked flabbergasted.

He was prepared for assassins or terrorists.

Guys in hoods with ragged eyeholes. Guys with foreign headdresses. Guys in American military camouflage garb.

But not for seven-foot-tall alien invaders with feet like T-rex and huge, razor-sharp blades on their elbows and knees.

Hard to believe the Hork-Bajir are gentle creatures when they don't have a Yeerk slug sitting in their cranial cavity controlling their minds and bodies.

Of course, these two Hork-Bajir were Controllers. They weren't gentle. And they were going to kill us both.

The Secret Service agent fired his gun.

I ducked back behind the curtain. Hoped he could hold them off for the short time I needed to finish the morph.

I closed my eyes and concentrated, willing the pace of the morph to accelerate.

CREEEEEK!

My face cracked open. Mouth stretched wide into a macabre grin. Nose spread. Ears migrated. Grizzly bone, muscle, skin, and fur emerged and layered.

My slim human shoulders hulked up and out. Too huge for my human spine to support. My back began to buckle.

My thick, curved claws were still growing when I stepped back out from behind the curtain.

The Secret Service agent had taken cover behind a desk. His face was white, his hand tight around his pistol.

The only reason he was still alive was that the Hork-Bajir had gotten tangled up in all the little chairs and desks that lined the hallway. Skinny-legged French-gilt jobs or something that now lay splintered on the floor.

"Andalite!" The Hork-Bajir paused. Not sure what to do next.

The Yeerks think the six of us are Andalites, the aliens who invented the morphing technology.

But only one of us is Andalite. Aximili-Esgarrouth-Isthill. Younger brother of War Prince Elfangor-Sirinial-Shamtul. Ax was a cadet in the Andalite Military Academy when he got dropped down in the middle of this war.

The rest of us are humans. Make that four humans and a red-tailed hawk.

Tobias.

The one who was lying dead outside.

I stood up on my back legs and screamed.

Only it didn't come out as a scream. It came out as an earsplitting grizzly roar that was enough to drain the last tiny bit of color from the Secret Service agent's face.

I looked at those two massive Hork-Bajir and didn't see victims of the Yeerk invasion. I saw murderers.

I saw killers.

And I saw blood.

I dropped down on all fours and loped toward them.

Dracon fire singed me but I didn't even feel it.

When I jumped, I brought both of them down with one tackle. Blades scraped me. Tore though my fur, into my flesh.

But I paid no attention. Nothing could hurt worse than the pain in my head — and my heart.

Then, suddenly, something grabbed me, pulled me away.

A gorilla. Full grown. Marco, in his favorite battle morph. I snarled, turned on the hulking primate. But he shoved me off balance.

I watched Jake in tiger morph and Cassie in wolf morph rush in to finish the fight.

One of the Hork-Bajir managed to jump up and escape through a window.

I was furious!

This was my fight and I'd been winning. Why couldn't Jake and Cassie find their own Controllers to kill?

Jake pinned the other Hork-Bajir. He bit his shoulder hard and then released him.

The Hork-Bajir leaped to his feet and followed

his buddy out the window, escaping in the direction of the Rose Garden.

I heaved myself to my feet and bellowed.

<What's the matter with you? That's two you let get away!>

<Stop it, Rachel,> Jake ordered calmly. <Cassie, you and Marco get to the Rose Garden. They're trying to get the President to the chopper, but there are Taxxons all over the place. I'm hoping those bleeding Hork-Bajir will distract them for a few seconds.>

Taxxons. Huge, voracious centipedes. They'll eat you — dead or alive.

<I'll go!> I raged as Cassie and Marco ran off. <I'll take care of the Taxxons. Let me go!>

<Uh-uh. You're out of this now. You're hurt bad. And you're so out of control you don't even realize how bad. That's why we pulled you off. Morph out, Rachel. Now.>

Jake turned away, an enormous Siberian tiger in a White House hallway.

Something about the way he just took it for granted that he could tell me what to do, tell me when to fight, when to back off, control me when one of the people I loved most was lying dead on the ground . . .

Something about it made me beyond angry.

Nobody told me when I was out of a fight. Nobody.

Not even Jake.

Why did he think he could do it?

Because I let him think he could. That's why.

Maybe it was time to show him he couldn't.

I'd rough him up. Not much. Just enough to let him know that I could take him. Any time. Any place.

I stood quietly on my back legs. He didn't hear a thing. He was listening for sounds outside. Trying to gauge his next move.

I was just about to jump him when Cassie came tearing down the hallway.

<Jake! We need you. Marco's down. They've got the President in the chopper. But they can't take off.>

<I'm going out there,> I announced.

<Rachel! No! You're covered in blood. The Taxxons will be all over you,> Cassie cried.

I wasn't afraid. Let them attack. I would tear them apart and enjoy it.

<Rachel! No!>

I bounded through the broken window toward the sound of chopper blades.

Toward pandemonium.

CHAPTER 3

The President was the prize in a serious game of tug-of-war.

Secret Service agents inside the helicopter were trying to pull him in.

A Hork-Bajir-Controller was trying to pull him out.

At least ten Taxxons writhed and hissed and hungered for blood.

Several Hork-Bajir hung onto various parts of the chopper, attempting to prevent it from lifting off.

One Hork-Bajir did a chin-up. The chopper blade took his head off.

Horrible.

The head rolled across the lawn, and five of

15

the Taxxons followed in a frenzy, dizzy with the excitement of fresh meat.

The other five Taxxons closed in around the chopper. Tore at the Hork-Bajir body. Their weight caused the chopper to dip. The Hork-Bajir with a grip on the President's leg stumbled.

I plowed in like a tackle!

Broke up the line of Taxxons.

Slapped away the Hork-Bajir body.

Yanked two more Hork-Bajir from their grip on the chopper blades.

Now the chopper could take off.

I heard the blades whir. The wind whiffled my fur as the chopper carrying the President rose over my head.

Now the aliens focused their attention on me.

I stood strong. Bleeding and roaring. Slicing and biting at the air as they came at me.

One after another they fell.

I was blind with killing rage.

Blindly efficient. A machine.

And then, suddenly, all was quiet.

The only sound was my own panting. The plop-plop of blood dripping from my muzzle.

I ruled! Was surrounded by dead Hork-Bajir. Watched a retreating band of Taxxons.

The roar of a tiger alone is enough to frighten most people to death.

But I'm not most people.

<I told you you were out!> Jake growled.

<Nobody tells me I'm out!>

We circled each other.

<This is a team, Rachel. A team. Do you know what that means?>

Jake bared the tiger's deadly fangs.

Big deal!

A grizzly can take a powerful amount of biting. Jake could sink those tiger teeth three or four inches deep and still not penetrate the shaggy bear coat.

<This used to be a team, Rachel. But you've turned it into a pack. Okay. Have it your way. You want to lead the pack, you're going to have to fight me for control.>

<I'll fight you,> I answered, rage making my voice thick. <I'm happy to fight you. Thrilled.>

I dropped my front paws to the ground and ran.

He didn't expect it, didn't really think I'd do it. I caught him off guard, rammed him in the ribs.

He let out a snarling cry of surprise and flew several feet across the yard.

But tigers are cats. By the time he hit the ground, his feet were underneath him and he was gathering his body for a spring.

I tried to move, but he was too fast!

He landed on me, and I fell sideways. I was sure I could knock him off, but he held on.

I flailed, twisted. But I couldn't dislodge the tiger.

<You can't take me, Rachel,> Jake said, voice oddly calm. <You're bigger, but you're not thinking clearly.>

<I'll show you who's not thinking!> I cried.

But I could feel the life seeping out of me.

<You're bleeding to death, Rachel. It's over. Now demorph.>

<NO!>

<If you don't demorph you'll die,> he said. <Face it, Rachel. You've lost. You lost this fight before it started.>

It was his calmness that sent me further into a blinding, screaming, homicidal rage.

He was so arrogant! So sure of his own superiority!

I thrashed! I screamed! I roared!

But he was right.

I was losing.

<Morph, Rachel!> Cassie. <Morph, now!>

But I didn't. And I wouldn't.

Because at that point, I knew I'd rather die than lose.

<Come *on*, Rachel!> Marco's voice broke. <Morph, Don't be stupid.>

A drop of blood from a torn ear trickled down my cheek. My neck. It tickled and caused me to jerk my eyes open and sit up with a scream that probably woke up everybody in the house.

Sweat, not blood, was trickling down my face.

I wasn't on the lawn of the White House.

Not in Washington, D.C., our nation's capitol.

No. I was in my own bed. At home.

And I'd been having a nightmare.

Again.

CHAPTER 4

"Where's Cassie?"

Marco sat at the keyboard of Ax's souped-up computer.

"I don't know. Did you look in the barn?"

"Yeah. Not there."

Cassie's barn is where we usually meet. Home of the Wildlife Rehabilitation Clinic.

Ax looked at me. <You seem unusually eager to speak to Cassie. Is there something you feel can only be discussed with her? Or can we help?>

Ax is Andalite. Not human. Technologically brilliant, but emotionally thick as a brick.

Or at least that's the assumption we go on. Don't ask me why. Because it's usually Ax, who, in his own strange way, seems to understand what's going on beneath the surface.

I threw myself down into the beanbag chair Marco had dragged to Ax's scoop when he realized he was going to be spending a lot more time there from now on.

Reality check: Marco is officially dead. He lives with his parents — also officially dead — and the free Hork-Bajir. Sometimes with Ax. He doesn't go to school anymore. He wouldn't be on a class trip.

I should have known the dream was a dream.

"There's really nothing in particular I want to talk about," I lied.

Ax looked at me and held his gaze for longer than necessary. He knew I was lying. Then he turned to peer at the computer screen over Marco's shoulder.

Okay, so I did want to talk to Cassie about something in particular.

Alone.

Cassie's the only one of us who might really be called "sensitive." Marco, like Ax, is perceptive. But that's not the same thing as being sensitive.

Besides, Marco has a way of making everything I say or do seem reckless. No way was I going to confide in him.

But I did need to talk. I was getting a little

21

worried about these nightmares. The same thing over and over.

Me and Jake. One-on-one. A final showdown.

Jake is our leader. I respect him. I don't always agree with his decisions, but he's in charge and I'm not. And that's the way I want it.

Especially after my one disastrous attempt at playing general. When I stupidly let Cassie get captured by the Yeerks.

So why the dreams?

"Wow!" Marco sat up and stared intently at the screen. "Look at this. On the Net. An 'I was there' first-person account of an alien attack on a nuclear sub. And here's another one. Some guy who doesn't want to be identified. He says he's a human-Controller whose Yeerk has joined the resistance."

<It would seem that the human race is about to learn the truth,> Ax said thoughtfully. <If the Yeerks no longer feel their presence is a secret, this could be the moment they decide to declare open war.>

"Woo-hoo!" I pumped my fist.

Marco shook his head in disgust. "Could you at least try to act like you're not thrilled at the prospect?"

Sometimes it's really hard not to like Marco. This wasn't one of those times.

"Look," I said, "covert war stinks. It's a nasty,

underground kind of thing that screws up your head. Look at what it's done to us. Look at the moral compromises we've had to make. You guys act like I'm some kind of psycho. But all I want is a fair fight. And you can't have a fair fight with an enemy that won't declare war!"

I was semi-breathless when I finished with righteous indignation.

But also with a kind of shame.

Ax and Marco were giving me that big-eyed look. The kind of look that clearly said they didn't believe what I was saying and were pretty sure I didn't believe it, either.

"I mean it," I insisted.

Lame.

I looked up at the branch overhead where Tobias was perched. His eyes fixed me with an intense stare.

Now remember, Tobias is a hawk. So he's always intense and staring.

But this time there was something in his stare that looked embarrassed. For me.

It was Marco who broke the silence. "I don't think any of us should fool ourselves. If this war is exposed, we're out of it."

Ax blinked. <What do you mean?>

Tobias rustled his feathers and tightened his talons on the branch. <Because if the Armed Forces get involved, we'll be pushed aside like

some kind of freak show. You know, kids who can do their own stupid pet tricks.>

"And that's fine with me." Marco smiled, folded his hands behind his head. "I'm ready to be pushed aside. I am ready to try normal again. Go back to school, graduate, get a good job, get married, have kids. I'm just living for the day when we can hand this over to the people who know what they're doing and who actually *like* doing it."

"I'd say we've done pretty good for people who don't know what they're doing," I snapped.

Silence. Three sets of eyes stared at me. Okay, four — because Ax has two sets of eyes.

I felt my face turn hot and red. I knew what the nightmares were about. Why had I been trying to fool myself and pretend that I didn't? I wasn't fooling anybody else.

My deep, dark secret was like an elephant in the living room.

A big purple one. With polka dots.

Nobody talked about it.

But everybody knew it was there.

The secret was that whatever we'd been doing, I did like it.

And the good guys aren't supposed to like it.

CHAPTER 5

I wheeled in a circle. Examined the ground for signs of Yeerk activity.

I'd gotten over feeling embarrassed and now I was peeved. Which is a polite way to say I was ticked off.

<You okay?> Tobias asked, flying near but not close enough to arouse suspicion if we were being observed from the ground. A bald eagle and a red-tailed hawk are not usually flying buddies.

<No,> I said in my surliest tone.

<Want to talk about it?>

There was a long pause.

<*Can* you talk about it?>

<I'm not trying to be mean,> I said quickly.

25

<All I really meant was that I don't want to lay something on you that you can't handle.>

Tobias turned below me.

<Gee. Thanks for knowing me so well. Look, Rachel. I can handle it. What's going on?>

<What's going on is that I'm sick of everybody acting like I'm some kind of warmonger, when all I am is ready and willing to do my duty. Marco whines and slacks every chance he gets. So how come I get that bug-eyed look from everybody and Marco doesn't?>

<That's not really fair,> Tobias said quietly. <Marco carries his weight and you know it.>

<Okay. So he's not a slacker. But he is a complainer. I'm sick to death of all that "Why me? Why us?" stuff all the time. How come everybody lets him get away with it?>

Tobias came up beside me, riding easy on a thermal.

<I think it's because Marco is just saying what everybody else is thinking but would never actually say.>

<Right. So how come everybody doesn't tell him to can the complaints and get on with the job? How come I'm the bad guy?>

<The others may not say the things Marco says, but basically, everybody feels the same way he does. They really don't want to be a part of this. On the other hand, nobody really under-

stands where you're coming from and . . . Never mind.>

He broke off and glided downward and away.

<And what?> I pressed, following.

Tobias didn't answer.

<You said you could handle it,> I reminded him.

<Okay. Okay. I don't think anyone really understands where you're coming from, Rachel. You're too into it and for a while we were all right with that. But now, it's starting to freak everybody out.>

Tobias poured on the speed and shot past me.

<Would it gross you out if I had a little dinner?> he said suddenly.

He didn't wait for an answer, but went screeching downward, talons raked forward.

I watched him close in on the rat. I felt even more isolated than usual.

Was he right?

Did the others think I was some kind of bloodthirsty sadist they were only willing to put up with because they needed me?

Were they really starting to dislike me as much as I was beginning to think they did?

I watched Tobias scoop the rat and head off for a distant tree.

I felt a shiver of revulsion.

Then anger.

Where did Tobias get the nerve?

Where does a kid that's a hawk that eats rats get off talking about *me* creeping people out?

And as far as my being into it? My liking it? Did they really think Jake didn't?

Maybe Jake didn't like the bloodshed. But the larger battle?

Of course Jake liked it. Who wouldn't?

The thrill of command. The adrenaline. The victory!

I flew away, leaving Tobias to his dinner. In the distance, the red winking light of a radio tower seemed to beckon.

Marco might be speaking for Cassie, Ax, and Tobias. But not for Jake.

Jake wasn't a whining coward at heart, like Marco.

Jake wasn't overemotional like Cassie.

He wasn't withdrawn and passive like Tobias, or a blindly faithful follower like Ax.

Jake was like me. Strong, brave, and aggressive.

WAIT.

That's it.

Jake was threatened by me.

So threatened that he was turning the others against me.

Trying to demoralize me.

Trying to be sure I didn't take over.

I stabilized my flight path and corrected my course by lining myself up with the red light on top of the tower.

A few moments later, I saw the roof of my house below and veered away from my path.

Tried to veer away . . .

I couldn't.

Couldn't change directions. Couldn't change course.

I was flying right toward the radio tower. Toward the red light.

Turn, Rachel, turn!

But I couldn't do anything but continue to fly straight ahead.

Closer. Closer!

Something was wrong. Very wrong. It was like being in the grip of a tractor beam.

It was pulling me toward the tower. Toward the red light.

I was going to crash right into it.

I was going to crash.

And I was going to burn.

CHAPTER 6

"Rachel! Get up. Breakfast in five minutes."

I jerked awake.

Again.

My heart was pounding. My nightgown was wet with sweat.

I heard Mom thumping on my sisters' doors, waking them for school before running downstairs.

It was early. Not even light yet.

I threw back the covers and rolled out of bed. Tried to shake off the creepy postnightmare feeling.

The old nightmare within a nightmare.

Was it over now? Really over? Was I finally awake?

I walked to the window. Felt the cold floor under my feet. Pinched my arms. It hurt.

I looked out. In the distance, I saw the faint red blinking light on top of the radio tower several miles away.

The source of the image in my dream.

I changed into jeans, sneakers, and a T-shirt. Ran downstairs.

Bacon and eggs sizzled on top of the stove. The door that led from the kitchen down to the basement was open. I could hear Mom down there doing laundry, opening the lid to the washer and then closing it with a bang.

Mom's a morning person. Full of furious, noisy energy when everybody else is dragging around trying to keep their eyes open.

I turned down the fire under the eggs, opened the fridge, and poured myself some juice.

While I sipped, I pulled my nightmares apart, taking inventory. What was real? What wasn't real?

Yeerk references were starting to pop up on the Internet. That much was real.

But we all agreed that it didn't mean a whole lot at this point. On the plausibility meter, an alien invasion ranks lower than an Elvis sighting to most people.

But what if people *did* start to believe it?

What if this thing started to get some real play?

It probably would mean an escalation of the conflict.

If that happened, there was no way Earth could win. Not unless the Andalites came riding to the rescue. And we weren't really relying on that.

Or unless the Animorphs were willing to dramatically increase the numbers on our side. To give more people morphing ability.

That was dangerous. We'd tried it once.

The result was not pleasant.

The result was David.

David, who had been a kid just like us. David, who had turned traitor and tried to sell us out to the Yeerks.

David, who was no longer David because we had deliberately trapped him in rat morph and left him on a barren rock island with nothing but wind, rain, and other rats for company.

Suddenly, the sweet juice turned sour in my mouth. My appetite disappeared.

That usually happens when I think about David.

I can't help it. Every time the memory surfaces, I feel afraid and guilty.

What we'd done to David hadn't been fair. Though at the time it seemed the only solution. Short of murder.

Still.

The idea was Cassie's. She determined that forcing David to become a *nothlit* was kinder in the end than killing him.

Sometimes I wonder: Kinder for who? For David or for us?

Anyway, I'm the one who morphed a rat and went down into the dirt with David. The one who bit off her own tail to catch him in our makeshift trap.

It was a dirty job. Somebody had had to do it and, as usual, I'd been the one. I'd been the only one with the stomach to stay with David for the full two hours it took for him to lose everything. To cease to be a human. To become a rat. Permanently.

Actually, Ax did stay with me, to keep track of time. Maybe also to give me support.

And when it was over he told me he never wanted to talk about what we'd done. Ever.

I knew it was stupid to feel guilty. David had been a threat. Not just to us, but to the entire fight.

He wasn't a threat now. Maybe he wasn't even still alive. How long does the average rat live, anyway?

SNAP!!!

I jumped and juice splashed out of the glass.

"Mom?" I yelled, reaching for paper towels to wipe up the mess. "What's going on?"

"A rat!" she shouted. "I put out some traps last night and I just caught one. Rachel, honey, can you come down here and do something with it? You know those things make me sick."

I felt like I'd been slapped.

My mother knew nothing about my real life. About the Animorphs or the Yeerk invasion.

She wasn't trying to insult me.

But at that moment she was just one more person who thought that when there was dirty work to be done, Rachel was the one to do it.

Still, I ran downstairs.

The rat lay on the cement floor, its neck broken in the trap. I grabbed a cardboard box from a pile of trash, lifted the rat with a broom handle, and dropped it inside.

"Just take it out to the garbage, please," Mom said, shivering a little. Then she turned back to the pile of laundry she was folding.

I carried the rat upstairs, out the back door of the kitchen, and around to the front of the house.

The garbage cans were already out on the curb, waiting for the morning pickup.

It was light now. But I could still see the faint red flicker of the radio tower in the distance. In another few seconds, I wouldn't be able to see it at all. It would disappear into the light of day.

I looked up and saw Tobias circling overhead, dipping his wings in greeting.

My heart lifted a little. Some of the creepy depression receded.

But as he wheeled more and more slowly, seeming almost to be drawing a bead on me, I had a horrible thought.

Maybe Tobias wasn't circling overhead to say hello.

Maybe he had his eye on the garbage. He'd been having a hard time hunting lately — we'd had almost no rain for a month — and I'd been bringing him food from time to time.

At first, it had hurt his pride. But eventually, he'd accepted the food.

My stomach lurched. I threw the rat and the box into the garbage can and shut the lid with a bang.

I hurried into the house and let the door slam behind me.

There was a time when Tobias had hidden his feeding habits from me. A time when he had been ashamed of killing and eating. Unbearably humiliated at having, in hard times, to scavenge garbage and roadkill.

But Tobias had shed his inhibitions. Had learned to follow his animal instincts. And to do what he had to do.

Maybe Tobias wasn't the only one who'd faced up to himself.

Was that what my dreams were about?

Shedding my inhibitions. Following my instincts. Doing what I had to do.

Becoming the leader.

CHAPTER 7

School was the same old same old.

Teachers chatted with one another in the halls.

Girls giggled.

Guys punched one another in the arm.

Stupid stuff, but familiar.

Not to me.

Not anymore.

I felt like I was watching everyone from behind a Plexiglas window.

I just wasn't there. I couldn't relate, not to the teachers, the boys, the girls. I couldn't even pretend to relate.

I didn't know how much longer I could keep up the pretense that I was just another kid. Just another kid with nothing more important to worry about than zits and pop quizzes.

I felt like I was going to explode.

But I have some self-control. In spite of what Jake and the others think.

I wouldn't say or do anything that might blow my cover. I had no way of knowing who was a Controller and who wasn't. And there were more and more human-Controllers every day.

Chapman, our assistant principal, had been a Controller from the beginning. I watched him come striding down the hall with a bunch of guys from the soccer team. Were they Controllers, too? Members of The Sharing?

They walked past me without a glance. By the time they turned the corner, I was in a fever of impatience.

If those guys were Controllers, we needed to be flushing them out, fighting them. Maybe even rescuing them somehow. Not playing wait and see.

Every hour, every day, we were missing opportunities to resist. To fight. To attack.

The Yeerk presence was spreading and we were still playing a game of defense.

Was that the right strategy?

I wasn't convinced that it was. And I'd told Jake that. More than once.

I looked over my shoulder. Every face I saw suddenly had Yeerk written all over it.

Jake came out of a classroom, cutting the corner close.

"Hi," I said, preparing to stop and talk.

He gave me a curt nod and walked on.

We play it cool at school. Avoid hanging out together much. Giving the wrong people the opportunity to speculate.

But I couldn't help wondering.

Had Jake's nod been just a little colder than usual?

Was there something less than friendly in the way he had walked right past me?

Was he still mad at me because I'd disobeyed him at the White Ho . . .

Hold it!

I shook my head.

The whole White House thing had been a dream. I hadn't disobeyed Jake's orders. I hadn't tried to kill him.

I hurried on to class and took a seat behind Cassie. I felt unsettled, uneasy.

She turned. "Hey!"

Her smile was genuine and I smiled back.

Or at least I tried to. But the sense of something being wrong was even heavier, more oppressive than it had been that morning.

Was this still a nightmare?

The bell rang. Kids threw themselves into seats, and the teacher strode to the front of the room, brisk and impatient to get started.

"Open your books to page two sixty-three," she said. Vaguely, I was aware of her launching into a lecture about Edgar Allan Poe. About the short story we had read last week.

"The Tell-Tale Heart."

I looked down at my book. Flipped through the pages. Tried to locate the passage the teacher was referencing.

I heard the click-clack of chalk on the board. Looked up to see what she was writing.

But I was blinded by the red glare that covered the entire front of the classroom.

Nobody else seemed to notice. All around me kids were looking at the board, busily copying the notes written there.

I looked behind me to locate the light source. Nothing.

I looked to the front again.

The red glow was gone. I could clearly see the teacher and the words she had written on the board.

My head began to swim. What was going on?

I was close enough to the wall to lean my head against it. The plaster felt cool and smooth against my cheek.

But inside the wall, I heard scratching and scrabbling. The sound of little claws.

Rats.

My hands began to shake. I balled them into fists to stop the trembling.

Maybe it wasn't so bad to be a rat if there were no people around to make you feel like a rat. Maybe it wasn't so bad if you lived in a place where everybody was a rat.

Behind the smooth plaster, scrabbling and squeaking. Then — I knew my mind was playing tricks on me. Or was it?

Someone was calling out to me from inside the wall.

Someone was crying, "Help me! No! No! Don't do this to me!"

It was David.

David was calling to me!

No!

"Rachel? Are you feeling ill?"

The teacher's kind voice penetrated the screeching alarm in my head.

Every face, including Cassie's, turned to stare at me. I realized I was leaning my head against the wall, my hand over my face like someone in pain or distress.

I sat up straight, swallowed hard.

"No," I managed to answer. "No, I'm fine."

"Why don't you excuse yourself for a few min-

41

utes," she urged. "Get some water and then come back when you feel better."

Probably afraid I was going to hurl and didn't want me to do it in her classroom.

Can't say I blamed her.

I picked up my books.

Cassie's lips moved slightly. Formed silent words of concern. What's wrong?

I shook my head. Nothing is wrong. Please stay put.

I got to the door of the classroom. Heard the teacher launch back into her lecture about "The Tell-Tale Heart."

A story about how guilt drives a murderer insane. Maybe more insane than he already is. It's the beating of the victim's heart that does it. The beating of the victim's dead heart, buried under the floorboards. Haunting the murderer. Thumping in his ears and his alone.

The sound pursues him.

Until he breaks. Until he confesses to his crime.

I did go to the water fountain. My mouth was dry.

I leaned over to sip. Reminded myself of all the reasons why I didn't need to feel guilty about David.

I — we — had had no choice. Even Jake had agreed that there was no choice.

"Why do you care what Jake thinks?" a voice behind me said. "A leader learns to live without approval."

I choked on the water. Stood up and whirled around.

Who'd said that?

Who?

There was nobody behind me.

I looked up and down the hall.

No one in either direction.

Was I dreaming?

No.

I was just losing my mind. Or what was left of it.

I pulled a piece of paper out of my notebook and scribbled a note to Cassie. Asked her to meet me in the barn after school. I found her locker, shoved the note through the vents, and headed for the exit.

School was just not a good place for me to be just then.

CHAPTER 8

I killed most of the rest of the day in the mall. A couple of hours of shopping and I felt almost normal again.

By the time I headed for the barn, I was feeling kind of silly. What was I? A little kid? Why was I letting a few bad dreams rock my world?

I was about twenty yards from the barn when I heard the scream.

Half a second later, Cassie came running out of the barn. About two hundred rats streamed behind her.

Rats!

This was a dream.

It had to be a dream!

Cassie was fast, but the rats were faster. They

climbed up her legs, scampered over her shoulders, down her arms. Biting. Scratching. Chittering madly.

Cassie's face began to melt. She stumbled to her knees. She was going into a morph. Momentarily helpless! The rats became more frenzied. It was horrible.

I didn't know what to do! What morph did I have that could take on two hundred rats and kill them all before they chewed Cassie to a pulp?

Whatever, just morph, Rachel! Go grizzly!

That's when the second rat pack came running out from the underbrush.

They attacked me!

Before I could even begin the morph, they streamed up the legs of my jeans, across my chest, down the collar of my jacket.

There was nothing I could do to stop them!

Or was there?

"Go to the pond!" I screamed to Cassie. "Run run run run!"

I took off.

Rats are small, but try running with fifty of them hanging on to you by their teeth like fishing weights.

Sharp little claws penetrated the skin of my arms and back. Sharp little teeth sank into my cheek.

"Stop it!" I screamed. "Get off me!"

The pond was only a few yards away. I didn't stop to kick off my shoes, rip off my jacket. I just plowed into the water.

The rats could hang on, but not for long. Not if I went under and held my breath. A rat's lungs are a lot smaller than mine. The rats would have to let go or drown.

I sank beneath the surface.

Some gave up almost immediately. Others dug their teeth in deeper, desperate.

I thrashed, flung wet rats off into the dark of the pond.

Were they swimming to safety? Were they drowning?

I didn't care. Just wanted to make them to go away!

By the time my lungs started to feel hot, the last rat had let go.

I was free. Except for the heavy, inert weights inside my shirt and jacket. Drowned rats.

Lungs burning. Time to surface.

I pushed upward. Hoping Cassie would be there, waiting.

No!

Something closed around my ankle. Yanked me down.

My lungs were bursting. I needed air!

But whatever was holding on to my ankle was determined to drown me along with the rats.

I thrashed and flailed and writhed . . .

And then everything went black.

Unconscious. But at the same time, aware.

Floating. Drifting.

There. But not there.

Me. But not me.

A dream.

Another level of an ongoing nightmare.

A nightmare structured like an intricate, labyrinthine game.

And then I opened my eyes. Peered not through the water, but through a gloom.

My eyes began adjusting to the dim light.

Not a game board or a maze. A stage set.

Like something right out of *Phantom of the Opera.*

Very Gothic. Very Poe.

I was in a dungeon. A huge, cavernous dungeon with stone walls slick with damp and slime.

Candles flickered in elaborate wall sconces.

Spectacular cobwebs, some as large as bedsheets, hung like shredding drapes from the light fixtures and the walls.

Mice scurried in and out of the shadows. The place stank of rotten garbage and sewage.

Wildly, I expected to see coffins. Vampires just waiting for the sun to set so they could suck my blood, make me one of their own. Midnight killers . . .

Easy, Rachel. Concentrate. Use your senses, not your imagination.

Listen! A persistent sound, a trickling. And a dripping.

An answer to one of my questions. Not a crypt. I was somewhere in the sewer system. But how had I gotten here?

I'd stand up. Take a look around. Figure out . . .

Couldn't stand. Was in some kind of box. A cube situated on an elevated platform. Maybe a table.

And I was bunched up, squatting with chin on knees, hands at my feet. Not enough room to stand up straight. To fully extend my arms or legs.

I pushed the hair out of my face. It was wet!

My jacket. Still full of bloated dead rats? Awkwardly, I patted my side.

No.

Okay, this at least was good.

I touched the wall of the cube.

What was it? Glass? Plastic? A force field, too?

Couldn't fully lift my head. Rolled my eyes toward the top of the cube. Only a few inches away. It was secured with an enormous, old-fashioned padlock.

Could I break it? Could I break the walls?

No. Not with my own arms and legs. I'd have to morph something big. Like grizzly. Something that would let me bust out of this prison . . .

Unless the cube wasn't breakable by physical means. Unless I'd kill myself trying to break it.

Okay. Airholes.

I could morph bug, crawl out through one of the holes and . . .

Never mind.

My fingers trailed the floor of the box. It was covered with a fine powder. Awkwardly, I held my fingers to my nose and sniffed.

Insecticide.

Whoever, or whatever, had brought me here, had thought of everything.

Yeerks? Something told me no.

Not Yeerks.

CHAPTER 9

Footsteps.

I jumped, startled.

Clanging footsteps above me.

I rolled my eyes back toward the top of the cube.

A vaulted ceiling soared maybe thirty feet overhead.

At the top was a small manhole cover.

And leading from the cover was a rusted iron staircase that snaked down the far wall like a fire escape.

Once for the sewer workers.

Now for whatever lunatic had constructed this macabre den.

The two guys clanging down the staircase definitely did not work for the utility company.

They reached the bottom. Brushed the hanging cobwebs aside like they were parting a curtain. And approached my cube.

Two guys. Late teens.

Neither looked bright enough to be the mastermind behind this nightmare scenario. *Definitely not the brains of the operation, Rachel.*

One was tall and skinny. He wore dirty, torn jeans and a black T-shirt. There was a tattoo of a rat on his right cheek.

The other one was short and fat. He also wore dirty, torn jeans. But his T-shirt screamed The Grateful Dead in psychedelic swirls and acid-hot colors. Over that he wore a light blue windbreaker. His hair was pulled into a thin, greasy ponytail.

There is just no accounting for taste.

These guys were nothing. I could take punks like these.

These guys looked like they survived on a diet of Twinkies and 7UP.

They were mine.

I'd say nothing.

I'd wait for them to tell me what was going on.

What they wanted.

Who they were working for.

What they'd done with Cassie.

And then I'd make them sorry they'd ever messed with me.

Tattoo looked at Grease. "Here it is, man. Just like he said."

Grease looked around, nodded. "Yeah, dude. This is the place. So I guess now's the time. Now is definitely the time . . . I guess."

Neither of the punks looked at me. Not in the face, anyway.

This was so not their deal.

Then, whose? Whose!

Stay calm, Rachel. Stay calm.

Assess before you act.

Don't do anything stupid.

Grease reached into his jacket pocket. I saw now that it was bulging.

Slowly, carefully he produced . . .

A rat.

Of course. Of course.

Dreams of rats, rats in the walls, rats in the basement, rats in my shirt . . .

If you weren't such a harsh person, Rachel . . .

Gently, Grease put the rat down on the table or platform. Placed it right in front of me, just on the other side of the clear wall of the cube.

We were inches apart, me and the rat.

It was large.

A rat that gazed up at me with a strange intelligence in its little beady eyes.

A rat that looked at me as if it knew something important about me.

As if it recognized me.

I'll kill you! I'll kill you! I'll kill you!

One of its own . . .

If you weren't such a harsh person . . .

Of course. Of course.

<Hello, Rachel,> said the rat. <Did you miss me?>

I wasn't surprised.

I wasn't scared, either.

This was a dream. Just another dream.

I'd wakened from the others. I'd wake from this one, too.

"David," I said, feeling more curious than anything else.

I was smarter than any of you. . . .

<Surprised?>

"No," I answered truthfully.

I shifted, tried to find some way to be comfortable inside the cube. My right foot was falling asleep. My lower back was beginning to ache.

It was time to wake up.

<Scared?> the rat named David asked.

I was smarter . . .

"No," I answered, truthful again.

You can't judge me!

And then the rat chuckled.

<Oh, well, it's still early. And no, Rachel, this isn't a dream. You're not going to wake up. Not this time.>

CHAPTER 10

<Would you by any chance want to know how I got here?> David asked abruptly.

He scurried along the outside wall of the cube. Nose quivering. Malevolent, beady rat eyes shining.

Satisfying himself that I was really, truly trapped.

<Would you by any chance want to know what it was like after you abandoned me on that rock island? What it was like all those months alone? Barely surviving? Trying not to go crazy?>

Suddenly, and certainly, I knew this was not a dream.

Suddenly, I felt dread — heavy, leaden, and cold — draining down my limbs.

It has to work or we . . . all of us . . . we will have to become killers.

I didn't want to know David's story. Didn't want to hear anything he had to say.

I could imagine it all well enough. I had imagined it. Over and over. Even when I didn't want to. Even when I had tried not to.

And when I did imagine David's situation, when the grim images of isolation invaded my brain, I invariably broke out in a cold sweat.

David sat up on his hind legs, his little pink nose twitching in the air. Searching for food?

<You didn't have the guts to kill me, Rachel. So you left me on a rock and hoped that nature would do your dirty work for you.>

David hadn't asked who the mastermind of the plan was.

I felt a hot flush cover my neck and face. He was right. We had. David had zeroed in on the discomfiting truth.

<It was horrible, Rachel,> he went on.

His voice was controlled, but barely. In it I heard incipient mania. Madness.

<It was horrible being a rat with human intelligence. Do you know what that means? It means that every time I was forced to eat a piece of putrifying flesh, my human brain was revolted. Every single day, the rat's need to survive made

56

me do things my human brain found humiliating. Degrading. Gross.>

"I feel that way every time I eat in the school cafeteria," I said. Determined not to let him see he was getting to me.

<Leave the one-liners to Marco,> David snapped. <He's good at being funny. Sometimes. But you're good at dirty work.>

I recoiled.

Maybe David was perceptive. Maybe he just had a good memory.

<Yes, I'm smart,> he said.

As if he'd read my mind!

<That's what got me into trouble with you Animorphs in the first place. But it's also what saved my life on that island. And it's what's going to bring me back and put me on top.>

"What are you talking about?"

Even to my own ears my voice was thin. Uneasy.

<I'm talking about beating the Animorphs, the Yeerks, and the entire human race,> David said, gleeful now. <Life, like being the smartest rat on an island of rock and rodents, is what you make it, Rachel. You Animorphs thought you were condemning me to a fate worse than death. But I turned the experience into an opportunity.

An opportunity to develop my intelligence to an almost supernatural level.>

Suddenly, David the rat scampered in a circle. Then another, tighter. Faster. Then another. Like a rodent whirling dervish. Or like he was trying to throw off some bad feeling. Or a bad itch.

After about ten revolutions, he came to a rest. Once again facing me.

Briefly I thought of making a snide remark about his getting himself some Prozac or Lithium or whatever. But I kept my mouth shut.

David spoke. His voice breathless from the manic exertion.

<At first, the monotony, the loneliness, was unbelievable. Enduring day after endless day on that rock, exposed to the elements, alone except for thousands of other rats, marooned, somehow, like me. But I survived, Rachel. Oh, yes. And eventually I befriended a few of my more intelligent brothers and sisters. I promised to lead them off the island if they would bring me food and obey me. Long story short, they did. How could they not? They were compelled to obey. They knew a natural-born leader when they saw one. And now my forces are here.>

"Forces?" I laughed. He really was insane! "What forces?"

David laughed back, mimicking me.

<The forces of David. You see, I escaped the island with a few select lieutenants.>

"I thought rats couldn't swim."

They get stuck in your shirt, weigh you down. Terrify you.

<Some can. Some can't,> David said. <But it never came to that because not long ago a group of naturalists came out to the island to count the bird population. They came, of course, in a boat. You hadn't foreseen that possibility, had you?>

I hadn't.

<I was smarter than any of you.>

It hadn't occurred to any of us that anybody would find a reason to visit that godforsaken pile of rock.

<There was some miserable little species of bird on the island. Stupid birds, but their eggs were delicious. Anyway, while the naturalists were clopping around counting nests, I boarded the boat with my lieutenants and hid. A few hours later, we were back on dry land.>

David paused. If he was waiting for applause, he'd have a very long wait.

<I sent my lieutenants out to recruit,> he went on, voice growing more excited with each syllable. <They did an excellent job. I now have a force over two hundred strong. But I'm not finished yet. Oh, no. Do you have any idea how

many rats there are in the world, Rachel? Billions. Maybe trillions. And I will lead them all.>

Okay.

"So now what?"

<You saw what my forces can do, back at the
barn. With armies of rats, and a few more like
these two,> David said, gesturing toward the
punks with his twitching nose, <no one can stop
me.>

I looked at the two witless thugs. David's willing hands and feet. Maybe I could stir up a little
dissension.

"You guys realize you're working for a rat,
don't you?" I said.

Tattoo shrugged. "He pays good."

"He pays good?" I snorted. "What are you
talking about? He's a rat. You're working for
cheese?"

David laughed wildly. <A rat can go many
places a human cannot, Rachel. You should
know that. Into banks. Into businesses. Places
where money is kept. Lots of money. I steal it. A
few bills at a time. It's hard work but it's paid off.
Over the last few months, I've accumulated two
hundred and twelve thousand dollars.>

I saw Tattoo and Grease exchange a glance.
Tattoo swallowed hard. So did Grease. Just thinking about money was making them salivate.

<The money is safe in a place no human

could possibly find,> David said. To his two bud-
dies as well as to me. <And there's more where
that came from.>

"So what am I doing here?" I asked. "If you're
poised to rule the world, what do want with me?"

David laughed.

<Can't you guess? I want justice. I want po-
etic justice. I'm going to do to you what you did
to me. Trap you. Take away your freedom of
choice.>

NOOOOO!

David stopped his nervous twitching and pac-
ing. Came to sit perfectly still, tiny black eyes on
mine.

<I'm going to make you become a rat. Perma-
nently.>

CHAPTER 11

"That's not justice," I snapped. "That's revenge."

David sighed.

<That's what all criminals say when justice finally catches up with them.>

"I'm not a criminal."

I am not some kind of nut.

<Jake said there were rules, Rachel. Rules about using the morphing technology for good instead of evil. Rules about what you could do to people and what you couldn't. How come he wasn't worrying about the rules when he told you to do this to me?>

"Jake didn't tell me to do it," I argued.

David looked surprised. Well, as surprised as a rat can look, I guess.

<He didn't? You mean, you just decided to trap me all on your own without orders from Jake?> His voice was condescending. <Wow. I'm surprised at you, Rachel. I thought the *Animorphs* were supposed to be so disciplined.>

I didn't know what to say. What I wanted him to know. The plan had been Cassie's. But we'd all agreed to it. Each one of us. And each one of us had had a part in it.

Was I any more guilty because I'd done the physical dirty work?

I'd had no choice! I was the logical one for Jake to send along with David. David hated me most. He wanted to humiliate me. And I'd allowed him to, for our own ends.

There's something pretty dark down inside you, Rachel.

"I did what I had to do," I said, trying to hide my distress beneath a tone of conviction. "When you were threatening us. When we thought you'd killed Tobias. Jake sent me after you because he knew I would do what was necessary."

You, Rachel, you love it. It's what makes you so brave. It's what makes you so dangerous. I don't know what will happen to you if it all ends someday.

Jake.

63

Neither one of us had exactly distinguished ourselves over the David episode. Not me. Not Jake.

<You think you're a soldier?> David demanded. <Some kind of noble warrior? If you're a real warrior, then these guys are caped crusaders.>

David laughed. Turned to his two creepy henchmen.

<Let me tell you guys what the mighty Rachel here did to me. Put yourselves in my shoes. I'm a kid, okay? Then aliens steal my parents and, bam, my whole world is destroyed. I can never go home. Never see my parents again.>

That wasn't my fault! I cried silently. *We were only trying to help you!*

<Before I can even process what's happened, I get press-ganged into this group of kids. They lean all over me. They push me around. And when I try to stand up for myself, Rachel here holds a fork to my ear and threatens me. Later, she promised to kill me.>

I felt myself flush with embarrassment.

Tattoo looked at me, cocked an eyebrow, almost imperceptibly lifted a thumb. As if to say, "All right!"

He approved of what I'd done. He was ready to bond with me.

This did not make me feel any better.

David rolled onto his back. Waved his paws in the air. Whipped his naked pink tail back and forth.

<You crack me up, Rachel. You really do. You want credit for being some dedicated war hero when all you are is just another punk.>

Abruptly, David flipped over onto his feet.

<You're all hypocrites. All of you Animorphs. From Jake, the sanctimonious killer, to you, the psycho. But I don't care about Jake and the others. It was you, Rachel. You were the bad guy. You're going to pay for what they all did to me. And you're going to pay big time. I'm going to make you.>

"You can't," I said simply.

<Sure I can. Morph. Now.>

I shook my head.

<Morph to rat,> David repeated. <It's the only morph that'll do. No grizzly. No elephant. And if you try to morph to insect, you'll die. Of course, maybe you'd prefer to die than exist like I have. Rooting through garbage. An unwitting pariah.>

David signaled his thugs. They each drew a gun.

David placed his paws against the wall of the cube and leaned in toward me. His nose quivered faster and his voice was gentle now.

Mockingly gentle and falsely comforting. <Look at it this way, Rachel. Living the rest of

65

your life as a rat isn't the worst fate imaginable for you. You'll still be able to fight. Rats are always fighting. Predators, enemies, other rats. It doesn't matter. As long as there's blood. That should be some consolation.>

I am not some kind of nut!

David's gentle tone turned nasty. <If you can't be a human bully, you can at least be a rat bully.>

"I'm not a bully."

I am not some kind of nut. I know what I'm doing.

<Sure you are. You loved poking that fork against my head and threatening my family. You got off on terrorizing a poor kid who'd basically lost his whole life. If you weren't a bully, you'd have been ashamed of yourself.>

I had been ashamed of myself.

But . . .

I still know where the line is. And I won't cross it.

But I never would have tried to kill David if it hadn't been for Jake.

You worry about me? What do you think you're going to do, Jake?

Jake had sent me to "take care" of David.

Everyone draws their own line.

He hadn't told me what, exactly, to do.

But he hadn't told me what, exactly, not to do, either.

So that was the same as giving me permission to do whatever it took to get the job done.

Wasn't it?

CHAPTER 12

<Oh! So it's Jake's fault after all?>

I jerked so hard I knocked my head on the ceiling of the cube.

David was reading my mind. Had he really developed some kind of supernatural intelligence, as he claimed?

Anthropomorphism.

That's when you slap human feelings, motives, behaviors on nonhuman animals. Or on trees or heavy machinery or anything at all not human.

It's sentimental. It's Nick Jr. I don't like to indulge in anthropomorphism.

But human-David was so present in rat-David,

I swear I saw actual human expressions flicker across the tiny rodent face.

Rat-David was smirking. Like he'd scored.

Rat-David was messing with my head.

Sinking the needle where he knew I was most vulnerable.

The only way to fight back now was to not react.

Not respond.

Not let him know how close to the mark he was.

"You can't outpsyche me," I blustered. "You can't outthink me. You're trying to tear me down. But it won't work."

<We'll see how much ego you have left when you're in permanent rat morph,> David snarled. <Morph to rat.>

"Or else, what?" I snapped. "Or else you'll kill me? I'd rather be dead than spend the rest of my life as a rat. I'd rather be dead than be a garbage-eating, money-pilfering, sewer-dwelling, rabies-carrying rodent."

I spit the words at him.

David jerked his head, as if he had been slapped. All his bravado seemed to evaporate. His whiskers drooped. His tiny shoulders sagged. He lifted one delicate paw to his face, as if to hide a tear.

A strangely human and humanizing gesture. David was crying.

Suddenly, he didn't look like an archcriminal. Some freaky Rat Man from a Saturday morning cartoon. Now he was Stuart Little. Just a harmless little rat with pink skin showing prettily beneath his white fur.

A helpless little creature that somehow had managed to survive on his own against all odds.

Not just survive, but prevail.

In a strange, twisted way, a valiant little creature.

Every sob was like a punch to my stomach. I felt awful. I felt cruel.

What was I doing?

Why was I trying to make him ashamed of something he couldn't help?

Why was I trying to make him ashamed of being something I had made him?

"David . . ." I began, trying to make my voice gentle.

Maybe there was some way to work this out. Some way to bring David back from the other side. Some way to give him a fresh start.

But he cut me off.

<You are already a *nothlit*,> he said quietly.

"What?"

<You stopped being human long ago, Rachel. No human could have done what you did to me. I

70

wasn't evil, Rachel. Just — troubled. Now, it's my turn. I said you'd pay. And today's the day.>

From some unseen source, a red light began to glow, illuminating the other side of the room. Revealing, out of nowhere, like a magic trick, a second cube on another platform.

There was someone inside the cube.

Cassie!

The cube was small, like mine. Padlocked. Only there were no airholes. And it was sound-proof. Cassie's mouth was moving. But I couldn't hear her, not really. Just faint, muffled cries.

David's thugs chuckled and pointed.

<It's not morph to rat or you die,> David said. <That choice would be too easy. No, Rachel, the choice is this: Morph to rat or Cassie dies. Of suffocation.>

Shrill laughter assaulted my ears.

I burned with fury.

Had I really felt sorry for this piece of crap?

David was right. We should never have stranded him on the island. We should have killed him when we had the chance. I'd known what he was. Way more than just a troubled kid.

But killing David had seemed over the top. Barbaric.

The reality was that I'd been afraid. Afraid to kill.

We all had.

I saw now that I, at least, had just been weak.

My hands clenched and unclenched. If I got even half the chance again, I wouldn't hesitate.

There would be no more fear. No more weakness.

No more moral wavering. No more uncertain compromises.

I would kill.

David's laughter. The thugs' stupid chuckling.

And then there was another voice.

A weird giggle.

Where was it coming from?

Now the giggle became a cry. Now a phrase. Repeated over and over.

Cassie, pounding on the inside of her cube. Her mouth forming the words: "Don't morph! Don't morph!"

Begging me not to sacrifice my life for hers.

"Cassie, stop shouting!" I yelled, willing her to hear. "You'll use up all the air. Stop!"

But she didn't.

Grease walked over to Cassie's cube. Pressed his hideous face against the front wall and made a series of grotesque expressions.

Mocked her!

<Morph, Rachel,> David repeated. <Your best friend is quickly using up all the available air in that cube. I'd say she has about another two min-

utes before unconsciousness sets in. As soon as you morph, I'll open an airhole for her."

I knew David.

He'd let Cassie die if I didn't morph.

But if I did morph — would he really allow her to live?

I had to take that chance.

I closed my eyes and tried to concentrate. But it was hard.

So many competing emotions!

Pity. Guilt. Fear. Rage.

I am not some kind of nut!

Impossible to focus!

<Hurry up, Rachel.> David's voice. <These punks want to see somebody die. They like watching people suffer.>

Not just rage.

Pure unadulterated hate.

It coursed through my body like jet fuel.

I would morph to rat. I would pretend to cooperate.

And when I got the chance, I would kill David. I would kill him and his punks.

SCHWOOOP!

My arms retracted. My legs shrank. I was a big, unbalanced lump on the floor of the cube.

I looked down at my feet. They were shrinking, shrinking. Now popping out of my massive

73

sneakers. Now sprouting tiny claws where there had been fleshy toes.

Now the rest of me shrank. Fast. My skin grew loose and pink, then rapidly sprouted white hairs.

My nose — still human. But not for long. It disappeared. Was replaced by a button or nub of flesh, which then narrowed into the rat's snout.

My eyes — still human, still huge in the rat's small skull. Impossible! Suddenly, the sockets began to shrink. Faster than the eyeballs! Squeezing the eyeballs until I thought they were going to pop.

Finally, my eyeballs began to shrink. A perspective change. My tunnel of vision seriously narrowed. And I was looking at the world from about three inches off the floor.

The morph was complete. I was a rat.

No!

Grease set a digital clock right in front of me, just outside the cube wall. David stood on his back legs and rested his front paws on the clock.

<Two hours, Rachel. That's all it takes. Just two hours of hell and then, it's you and me. Rats together. Forever.>

CHAPTER 13

Two hours.

I had two hours.

And then my life might as well be over.

The rat's natural curiosity kicked in. I didn't try to stop it.

Maybe the rat's instincts for escape would pick up something I had missed.

Nose quivering, whiskers twitching, I ran along the four walls of the cube. Stopped to sniff at each corner. Stood up and pressed my front paws against each wall.

<There's no way out, Rachel. Do you think I would go to all this trouble and then build a prison you could get out of?>

I scurried back to where David stood, looking in. We were nose to nose. Eye to eye.

<Hungry, Rachel? Don't bother to answer. I know you are. Rats are always hungry.>

Tattoo came over to the cube. In his hand he held a plastic baggie. It was filled with rotted food. Methodically, he began to poke pieces of moldy carrots and green meat through the air-holes. Stinking, rotting garbage crawling with maggots.

<Stop!> I shouted.

<Just try it,> David coaxed. <Mold is not too bad once you get used to it. And the sooner you get used to eating garbage, the happier you'll be. It's what rats do. Unless, of course, you're me.>

Grease placed a chunk of fresh French bread next to David. A bunch of grapes.

<Luckily, I'm a genius,> David went on, casually poking at the bread with his twitching nose. <I've managed to rise above my station in life. Sure, I'm a rat. But I'm also the big cheese.> David looked at me and giggled. <Get it?>

Yeah, I thought. *Pure genius.* But I said nothing.

David didn't seem to mind my silence.

<Other rats have to forage for themselves. Not me. I have others do my dirty work. I don't like going into places where I know I'm hated. Do you?>

<I wouldn't know,> I answered swiftly.

Why had I spoken?

Given David more to use against me.

<Oh, I think you do, Rachel. I mean, come on. You know the others hate you. You know they'll be relieved you're gone. That you're not their problem anymore. That they don't have to worry about what wacko Rachel is going to do next.>

I think there's something pretty dark down inside you, Rachel.

<You don't know what you're talking about.>

I worry about you, Rachel. I don't know what will happen to you if it all ends someday.

<Oh yes I do, Rachel. You're a problem. The Animorphs can't control you. But they can't kill you, either. So my brilliant plan is the perfect solution.>

I looked over at Cassie. She was crouched, silent. David had kept his word. He'd instructed Tattoo to open an airhole. Cassie could breathe.

Was she breathing more easily because I was out of the way?

Was David right? Would Jake and Marco, Ax, even Tobias, be relieved?

Maybe they would. Maybe they wouldn't admit it to one another. But secretly, deep down, maybe they'd be relieved.

Whew. Rachel's gone. At least that's over!

I am not some kind of nut!

No! It was unfair! Unfair. Unfair. Unfair.

Since the beginning I'd only done what had to be done. What nobody else had wanted to do.

And was anybody grateful?

Grateful for all the sacrifices I'd made?

No.

<You see, Rachel, the problem with the Animorphs is that they don't appreciate you. And they don't appreciate you because they've never figured out who they are. Never really defined their goals. You can't achieve goals if you don't know what they are. Me? I know what my goals are.>

I tried to ignore him. I paced, sniffed, circled.

But there was no escape.

Not from the cube.

Not from his voice.

<I'm going to beat them all, Rachel. The Animorphs. Now, you're probably thinking that's crazy. How can I, a lowly rodent, defeat an experienced guerilla force with alien technology on its side? But let's put this in perspective. If a lowly slug can lead an intergalactic invasion, then surely a pair of rats — one of them a genius — could at least carve out a little kingdom for themselves.>

In spite of myself, I was curious.

<How?>

<If you wipe out the hosts, you can wipe out the Yeerks. Or at least scare them off the planet.>

<What are you talking about?>

<I'm talking about plague, Rachel. Bubonic plague. Black death. Rats carry plague. And rats can get in and out of a biological weapons lab with no problem. Labs where there are vials and vials of plague virus.>

<You'd wipe out the whole human race!>

<Not all of it. But a large percentage. Maybe half. And what's left, we could control by threatening more plague. Just think! I, David, a rat, would be the most powerful creature in the world. Armed with one tiny bacterium of bubonic plague, and an army of rats, I could be deadlier than a nuclear arsenal.>

All of a sudden, I realized that David wasn't crazy.

Well, maybe he was crazy, but his plan wasn't.

79

CHAPTER 14

The voice.

<We could win, Rachel. Rats could rule the world.>

I was smarter than any of you.

<Sure, we'd still be rats. I mean, we wouldn't be able to drive a Ferrari or eat at Le Cirque. But all humans would have to bow down and grovel to us. The human race would be at our disposal! Our beck and call!>

Le Cirque? I thought inanely. Ignoring the full import of David's message. Human-David had been more of a Wendy's kind of guy.

<The key to winning is no mercy, Rachel.>

David's voice was — grand. Somehow compelling.

Like he was one of those inspirational speakers big corporations hire. The ones who come in and pump up a flagging sales department into a slogan-induced frenzy of sell-sell-sell energy.

Still, what he was saying did make some sense. Hadn't I always been the one to preach "show no mercy"?

<We can't go soft, Rachel. We can't give in to emotional attachments. Or to morality. A leader leads because he or she is a law unto themselves. A leader really believes that law will be accepted without question by those whose destiny it is to follow.>

Yes, yes. A leader has to be totally focused, totally without mercy, totally sure of her decisions. . . .

<And if you were to destroy Jake, well, then, the other Animorphs would follow you without question. Right?>

The voice. It was hypnotic.

It made sense.

It was seductive.

It was reasonable.

It spoke to me.

<*Right,* Rachel?> he pressed gently.

Jake doesn't even know how to use his power.

<Right,> I heard myself agree.

Then a crazy laugh, high and wild, broke the spell.

And I realized it wasn't David's voice I'd been hearing.

Not David's voice that had manipulated me. That had cast its magic over me.

It was another voice entirely.

I shot a look at the clock.

What!

I panicked.

What happened?

Where had the time gone?

What had David done to me!

And then there was a low humming sound. Very faint, but audible.

And again, the dark, cavernous space was lit with an eerie red glow. Only now, the light source was visible.

The light source was a large red eye.

It hovered over the room from just under the vaulted ceiling. Peered down like a gigantic red spotlight.

Cassie. Pounding on the wall of her cube. Shouting. I couldn't hear her but I knew what she was saying.

"Demorph, Rachel. Demorph! Don't get trapped. Don't let them do this to you!"

I stared at David.

His nose and whiskers quivered.

He didn't look like a world ruler.

He didn't look like any kind of leader at all.

He looked like a scared little rat.

Some kid's science-class pet.

An exterminator's dream.

My brain kicked into overdrive.

<Wait!>

David cringed.

<No,> he protested softly.

I stood up on my hind legs.

<Reality check.>

<Everything I told you is true,> David said quickly. <I escaped from the island. I have a plan to rule the world. I . . . >

<Rats are not sentient creatures,> I interrupted. <They don't take orders. They don't organize. They can't be rallied like troops. And they don't attack people on command.>

David chittered and lay on his belly.

<You might be a rat with human intelligence but that doesn't make you Dr. Dolittle. You can talk to me and you can talk to your punks. But you can't "talk" to other rats.>

<You don't know what you're saying! You don't know anything!> David cried. <Shut up! Shut up!>

<Which means that what happened outside the barn couldn't have happened,> I went on, my brain whirring. <And what you said happened on

the island — your building a loyal following — couldn't have happened. Which means that this, right now, can't be happening, either!>

I looked over at Cassie.

She was smiling. And then Cassie wasn't Cassie. She became a creature we had encountered before.

The Drode!

An intergalactic trickster.

Two legs. Body held forward and balanced by a stubby tail. Like a bird or a small dinosaur.

Its hands were flimsy. Weak. Its head was vaguely human in shape. The eyes in that head, wide-set.

Intelligent.

Laughing.

Cruel.

The Drode.

The creature who'd once offered me a deal. Who'd called me "Rachel of the dark heart."

The Drode.

Sidekick to the most powerful and malevolent force in the universe.

A force that had vowed revenge when Jake doomed its childlike killers, the Howlers.

A force that could be balanced only by the Ellimist. A being whose powers were equally comprehensive. Whose motives were seemingly good.

But this was not the Ellimist. This was the force that had haunted Jake's dreams.

And now, I realized, mine, too.

<Crayak!>

CHAPTER 15

The Drode laughed harder. Then . . .
WHOOOMPPH!

Came popping up out of the cube like a Jack-in-the-box.

"You called my master's name. Can it be that you need some help, Rachel? Rachel of the dark heart. Rachel the soon-to-be *nothlit.* Rachel the rat."

<What are you doing?> I demanded. <What's this all about?>

<It's about payback,> David sniveled.

I laughed.

<You're telling me that the all-powerful Crayak is working for a rat?>

The Drode giggled.

<Rachel, Rachel. Who knew you had a sense of humor? No, Rachel. The rat works for Crayak. Whatever puny scores the rat has to settle are of no interest to us. No, we seek your help in a larger payback. We once told you we had hopes for you, Rachel. Do you remember? We still do.>

<What do you want?>

The red eye that was Crayak pulsed and seemed to grow some sort of extension from below. A body of sorts? Or a machine? A little of both or neither. Then Crayak spoke.

"I want to help you realize your full potential, Rachel. We have watched you. With interest and with growing admiration. Why are you content to follow when clearly you should lead?"

<So this is about Jake? I remember now. You told him he'd suffer for what he did to the Howlers.>

"No. This is about you, Rachel. You could be so much more than you are." It sighed. "What a waste it would be to see you finish out your days as a rat."

<I'm not worried,> I lied.

"We know you are brave." Crayak's tone was condescending. "But do not disappoint us by being a fool. Unless you want to become a *nothlit,* you need my help."

<I don't need your help,> I countered. <Because it's pretty clear that none of this is really happening. Do you think I'm an idiot?>

Crayak, the conglomerate of life and technology, chuckled. "What do you mean?"

<I mean this whole thing is an illusion. David's story. Rats can't be led like an army. They can't form alliances, and they can't decide to stow away on boats. Which means that David cannot be here. He is an illusion. And I seriously doubt that I'm a rat. Look, you're all just a nightmare. A seriously foul dream.>

"Excellent, Rachel. You are a skeptic. A good quality in a strategist. And a leader. David? You've had your fun but Rachel got the best of you. I told you that if she guessed there was more here than what meets the eye, you had to tell her the truth. Tell her.>

<I am here,> David admitted grudgingly. <But everything was Crayak's doing. I don't have a rat army. Rats don't understand much of anything. You can't talk to rats.>

David's rodent body fairly emanated rising panic. Hysteria. So did his voice.

<Do you have any idea just how bad it was for me on that rock, Rachel? Not another sentient creature. And having to defend myself from the others? From other rats? From birds of prey? From the rain and the cold and — >

"I didn't tell you to whine!" Crayak thundered angrily.

<Okay! Okay!> David turned to me. <Crayak got me off the island.>

<In exchange for what?> I asked.

<In exchange for a companion. I would have chosen Cassie. She was nice to me when no one else was. But that's why I couldn't choose her after all. I wouldn't condemn her to this living hell.>

The thing that was Crayak bulged and shrank. Was it breathing? Did it need to breathe?

"You see, Rachel," it said, "this isn't a nightmare. Or a bad dream. The reality is, Rachel, that you are, indeed, in rat morph. In a matter of minutes you will be trapped forever in the morph. You will live out your life as a rat with only this weak and sniveling would-be traitor as your companion."

In spite of myself I began to shake. The-human and the rat-me.

Crayak went on, it's voice low and powerful, like the rumble of thunder.

"I can free you, Rachel. I can free you from the cube. I can free you from David. I can free you from the morph. But first, you must free yourself from yourself."

I looked at the clock.

Twenty-two minutes!

<Stop talking in riddles!> I shouted. <I don't know what that means. Free myself from myself.>

The thing that called itself Crayak laughed. My heart thudded with the reverberations.

"It is time you found out."

There was no sound. But it felt like there should have been a sound. A WHOOSH! or a SCHLOOOOP!

Because in an instant everything was altered.

The cube was gone and I was human again. I stood in the center of the cavernous chamber.

David's punks were trapped inside Cassie's cube.

Cassie? I hadn't seen her since the Drode appeared.

Crayak had moved, somehow, to the far side of the room. Suddenly, from its bulk a muscled armlike thing extended.

"Come with me, Rachel."

I don't know why. But I reached out. And the distance between us magically shrank.

I looked up. And in an instant, the distance between me and the thirty-foot roof disappeared.

I looked down and saw a white speck scurrying into the corner for safety. David.

"What is this?" I demanded. "I'm a giant now?"

"Only if you need to be," Crayak replied. "You

are as strong as you need to be. As big as you need to be. As ruthless as you need to be. You're not Rachel anymore. You're Super-Rachel. Can't you feel it? The raw power?"

I could feel it. I could feel a strange and magnificent energy coursing up and down my arms and legs, like electrical currents.

The energy was potent. Intoxicating. Familiar.

I'd experienced it before.

The energy was hate. Hate now enhanced with outrageous power. And the moral certainty that I was right. That everything I thought and everything I did was right right right!

I felt like a god.

There was nothing I couldn't do. No one I couldn't destroy.

I stared at my hands. They weren't just hands. Not just pink flesh and coursing blood and pulsing muscle. They were powerful machines, reinforced with gears and pulleys and wheels.

I flexed my fingers. Steel claws extended from beneath my fingers. I flexed again and they retracted, disappearing into the flesh of my fingertips.

"Yes, Rachel," Crayak said. "There when you need it. Gone when you don't."

I looked down. The floor was the usual distance away. I was normal-sized again.

I heard the Drode giggle.

"Think fast, Rachel."

From the other side of the room, the Drode heaved what looked like a massive iron cube in my direction. It was big enough to flatten me like a bug.

Reflexively, I reached out my arms.

Every bizarre morphing sensation I had ever experienced was suddenly telescoped into a nanosecond.

Every cell burst, shifted, flowed, exploded with energy! My body adapted to meet the needs of the moment.

I was twenty feet tall with the strength of thirty Hork-Bajir. My hands were massive steel claws.

I caught the cube easily. My "fingers" closed neatly around it as if it were a softball.

Even the Drode looked slightly amazed.

I dropped the cube with a thud and lifted my lip in a snarl. I felt my teeth click together. Upper and lower rows had become iron fangs that sparked as they gnashed against each other.

"You!"

The Drode turned to run.

CHAPTER 16

But it was too late.

I leaped, my long, strong legs propelling me across the huge room in one fluid motion.

I was on it in a heartbeat.

One hand closed over the Drode's body. The other over its head.

With the effort it would have taken a ten-year-old to peel a banana, I tore its head from its body.

A flood of euphoria and adrenaline surged through me.

No one could stop me!

Nothing could resist me!

No army could defeat me!

I was a superpredator. A superhero.

I was free of any human weakness.

Free of any fear.

This is what Crayak had meant about freeing myself!

Now I understood!

"I am free!" I shouted gleefully. "I am free!"

My voice was a monstrous roar echoing through the dungeon-like sewer.

Crayak laughed.

"Not so fast, Rachel. You are not free. Because you still believe this to be a fantasy, don't you? A silly simulation that gives you the illusion of deadly power. Like one of those video games you humans enjoy so much. A virtual-reality experience."

Something in my palm vibrated like a pager.

It was the Drode's head. Laughing.

The Drode was still alive.

Grinning up at me with its green-rimmed smile.

Rachel, do you feel the adrenaline rush of murderous desire? Do you feel the urge to reach out and destroy me?

"There are many masters of illusion in the universe, Rachel. Many manipulators of perception. But only I am a master of reality. A manipulator of the concrete. Well, then, perhaps this is a fantasy, after all. Your fantasy. But I can make it real at any time. For example, perhaps you would like to rip the Drode apart for real?"

"Hey!" the Drode protested. "Now, let's not get carried away."

You know, Crayak could use you, Rachel. If you ever find yourself desperate, Rachel. At an end. In need . . .

Suddenly, I was furious.

. . . the adrenaline rush of murderous desire . . .

I was tired of being toyed with.

Was this a fantasy or wasn't it?

A nightmare, a dream, a hallucination?

Crayak was deliberately confusing me!

I wasn't free of anything. Of Crayak, of my guilt, of David, of my fears, of anything!

I was still a prisoner!

Two hours of horror . . . reach out and destroy . . .

I took dead aim at the glowing red eye.

Hurled the Drode's head at it!

But the eye simply disappeared.

The Drode reassembled in midair and landed on its feet. Sighed and stretched its arms and legs to their full extent.

Crayak reappeared on the other side of the room.

"Rachel!" it chided. "That was a waste of

time. A waste of energy. A waste of power. You cannot harm me. You know this. Why make yourself appear foolish to your inferiors?"

It gestured toward David, cowering in the corner.

David squeaked. <Who are you calling inferior! No way am I inferior to Rachel. She's the same as me. Except she's been luckier.>

"Perhaps you are right," Crayak mused. "Perhaps I am the one wasting my time and energy."

This time, there was a sound effect. Or I imagined there was.

WHOOSH!

I was a rat again.

NOOOOO!

I was inside the cube.

Rotted food strewn at my feet.

And David was with me.

I looked at the counter.

No.

Who could save me? Who could I ask to save me?

Not Jake, not the other Animorphs. Not the Ellimist.

There was nobody I could turn to.

Nobody.

If you ever find yourself desperate, Rachel . . .

CHAPTER 17

I scratched at the walls.

It was horrible!

More horrible than before.

To be so small and so weak after experiencing so much strength and power.

Unbearable!

I was ready to do anything — anything! — to get it back. To get back the power.

The invincibility!

A voice. In my head. The Drode.

Something it'd said to me a long time ago. When we'd first encountered it.

Remember this: Your cousin's life is your passport to salvation in the arms of Crayak.

No . . .

I pushed away the memory.

David laughed.

<I've been waiting a long time for this.>

<Shut up.>

<I knew you'd never live up to Crayak's expectations,> David gloated. <I knew it would wind up like this. Because you're not any better than I am, Rachel. If I deserve this psychological, this emotional torture, you deserve it double.>

<Shut. Up.>

<Make me,> he taunted. <Let's see how tough you really are when you don't have your buddies or your grizzly morph to back you up.>

I turned and jumped him. Dug with my claws. Bit with my teeth.

But David was bigger and more experienced with the morph.

His back claws ripped at my belly. His teeth, needle sharp from months in the wild, sliced my face.

I was losing. Losing the fight.

Losing to David!

<NOOOOOO!>

Uncontrollable rage! Unbelievable hatred!

I was overwhelmed with adrenaline.

David had me!

I was pinned, couldn't move!

The counter turned over again.

<NOOOO!>

I thrashed with all four legs. Futilely, my tail whipped back and forth, back and forth.

<NO! NO! NO!>

The sound . . .

WHOOSH!

Suddenly, I was myself again.

Human-Rachel.

Outside the cube and crumpled on the floor. Flailing around like a two-year-old having a tantrum.

"Tsk, tsk." Crayak. "Is this how a leader should behave?"

I jumped to my feet.

SPROOING!

Steel coils in my knees and ankles.

Once again, I was Super-Rachel!

And the hatred I had felt toward David, the killing rage, was still pumping through my body. Throbbing through my brain.

My eagle eye caught the two punks.

Somehow they'd escaped the cube. Were climbing the iron staircase welded to the stone wall. Headed for the manhole cover in the ceiling.

Apparently, things had turned just a little too weird for them. Certainly Crayak hadn't taken pity and let them escape their prison.

Or had it?

Didn't matter.

I reached up and my arm ratcheted twenty feet.

Curled my fingers around a piece of the iron staircase and pulled.

The staircase came away from the stone wall as if it had been made of balsa wood.

KKKERRAAK!!!

Tattoo and Grease fell screaming through the air.

Crayak gestured gracefully.

From nowhere, a net spread about fifteen feet off the floor.

THUMP! THUMP!

And broke the punks' fall. For a moment the net swayed gently. Then it flipped and dumped the two punks out onto the floor.

They lay there at my massive feet, stunned. Stared up at me with terrified eyes.

"Imagine what you could do for the good of Earth with such powers," Crayak said.

The thought was enticing.

"Puny bullets would have no effect on you. Yeerk Dracon beams would only warm your flesh.

You could destroy anyone, anything, that you chose."

I tried to make my expression neutral.

Indifferent.

But every nerve ending in my body was vibrating with ambition.

"You would let me stop the Yeerks?"

Crayak waved a dismissive hand.

"I would create you, Rachel, and you would do as you please."

WHOOSH!

I was back in the cube.

A rat.

With David's teeth in my neck.

And the counter in front of my eyes.

We struggled! Tails, teeth, and claws.

The contrast was unbearable.

From absolute dominion to absolute submission.

Unthinkable! Unendurable!

I managed to pull my neck from David's grip. Felt the skin on the back of my neck tear.

I ran madly, senselessly around the cube.

David chased me.

If Crayak were going to create a supercreature, why had it chosen me and not Jake?

I couldn't take this anymore!

Salvation in the arms of Crayak . . .

<Don't worry,> David called from behind me. <Life as a rat won't be so bad. You won't have any strength. You won't have any power. And you definitely won't have any friends. But you *will* have me.>

And the Drode laughed hysterically.

CHAPTER 18

ШHOOSH!

I was Super-Rachel.

Outside the cube.

Stumbling to my feet.

"Quit the yo-yo effect. I get it!" I screamed at Crayak. "I can be a rat. Or I can be a god. But only if I do what you want."

"What makes you think you know what I want?" Crayak asked. "How dare you presume to understand? Understand only this, Rachel. You and you alone decide what you will do. And you and you alone accept the consequences."

I took a deep breath and forced myself to sound calm.

In control.

"But you do want something. Don't you?"

Crayak chuckled.

"That's better, Rachel. Be cold. Do not let your emotions sway you. Yes. If I create you, if I make you the most powerful force on Earth, I will ask for something in return. Is that unfair?"

"It depends on what you want."

"I want justice," it said reasonably. "Jake destroyed my Howlers. Now I want you to destroy Jake."

"Never," I said, drawing in my breath.

"Rachel. Think! I'm offering you a chance to destroy the Yeerks once and for all. To save the life of every human on the planet. Are you willing to sacrifice billions of lives to save just one?"

The needs of the many versus the needs of one.

"You can't make me murder Jake."

"I can't *make* you do anything," Crayak reminded me. "You have free will. What you do with it is up to you. You can use it for good. Or you can use it for evil. Now, listen. Be sure you understand. I'm offering you a chance to save the world," Crayak said. "I'm offering you the chance to be a force for good — or for evil. What is it going to be?"

I closed my eyes, confused now.

Kill Jake and save the human race from being conquered by the Yeerks.

Make Jake a sacrifice. His death — the death of one human kid — would bring freedom to millions. Billions.

And I . . .

It was a deal with a devil.

And its name was Crayak.

"I'm one of the good guys," I said.

Then I tried to figure out exactly what it was that made me a good guy.

I had no answer.

Maybe I'd never had one.

Crayak chuckled again.

"Good guys. Bad guys. It seems so simple, and yet it is anything but."

I heard a sound. A cry for help!

Cassie!

Trapped again in the other cube and pounding on the front wall.

Calling out to me. Begging me to do something.

What?

What was she begging me to do?

"Good and bad are so simple for Cassie," Crayak said.

Yes. Yes. Cassie always knew right from wrong.

"So what is she telling you to do?" it asked.

I didn't know.

Would Cassie sacrifice herself to save the entire planet?

Yes. Without a second thought.

Would she sacrifice Jake?

I didn't know.

Would she sacrifice me to *nothlit* status to save Jake?

I didn't know that, either.

"What is Cassie telling you to do?" Crayak pressed.

"I don't know!" I cried. "I don't know. I'm confused."

"But good and bad are so simple," Crayak teased.

"Only for the simpleminded," the Drode mocked. Hopped up and down. Began to sing in a childish voice, "I'm one of the good guys. I'm one of the good guys. I'm one of the good guys!"

"The good against the bad," Crayak murmured. "The age-old battle. Let's settle it once and for all."

WHOOSH!

In the blink of an eye, the dungeon-like sewer expanded to the size of a football field. Bleachers lined three of the walls.

High up in the stands, I saw the pulsing red mass. Beside it, the Drode.

Crayak nodded, and the Drode threw something out onto the field.

It was a ball.

The ball hit the ground, bounced slightly, and rolled toward my feet. I bent to pick it up . . .

And reared back when the ball exploded into matter.

I found myself eye-to-eye with Visser One's Andalite eye stalks.

He let out a bellow of rage and surprise. Careened backward.

I did the same.

Tried to get over the shock of being suddenly face-to-face, one-on-one, with my most hated enemy.

Who was now galloping toward me. His lethal tail blade whisked the air, prepared to strike.

I kept my eye on the tail and ducked.

I was unprepared for the speed and velocity with which my body responded.

I shot across the floor on my stomach at an easy twenty-five miles an hour!

I hit the wall headfirst. Didn't feel a thing. The wall crumbled, buried me under a pile of rubble.

I could hear Visser One shouting at Crayak.

<Where am I? Who are you! And why have you brought me here?>

<I have brought you here to fight for your life,> Crayak replied calmly.

Visser One laughed. No mistaking, ever, that demonic sound.

<Well then. It would appear I have already won.>

Beneath the pile of bricks and stone, I smiled.

Looks are deceiving.

CHAPTER 19

I stood.

Rocks, stones, and debris fell away like dust.

I might as well have been covered with packing peanuts.

Visser One's main eyes narrowed. He looked up . . . up . . . up.

I couldn't even begin to guess how large I was.

But for the first time since this whole infuriating war began, Visser One looked like a very minor threat.

The visser studied me with his four eyes. But it was clear — he didn't suspect that I was one of the Andalite bandits that had been plaguing his efforts to take over the earth.

The visser wasn't afraid to tell everyone within ten miles what he was thinking. If he thought I was an Andalite in some bizarre morph, he'd be shouting words like "scum" and "fool."

But he was silent. It was also clear that he didn't even recognize me as human.

How could he? I was a massively distorted version of myself.

Then he laughed. A practiced, evil laugh.

<This is a trick. A hologram. Who is playing games with me? Do you know who I am?>

"Who are you calling a hologram?" I sneered. I reached forward, put my massive, machine-like hand on his chest, and shoved.

<ARGGHGHHHH!>

Visser One went flying. Tail flailing, legs kicking. He bounced off the wall on the far side of the room. Crumpled to the floor, delicate Andalite arms crushed beneath his chest.

He lay still for a full minute. Then slowly he struggled to right himself.

A red spotlight illuminated the floor of the arena. Crayak, hovering above us. Part biology, part technology. All destructive.

"I am Crayak," it said to Visser One. "I think you know of me."

Visser One choked out his answer. <Yes. I have heard of you. But I did not really believe you existed.>

"I exist," Crayak said simply. "And I have a little job for you, Yeerk."

Visser One puffed out his chest. The effort seemed to cost him. His Andalite body was that of a seasoned warrior, but no warrior on this planet or any other could come up against me.

<A little job!> he spat. <Are you aware that I lead the Yeerk invasion of Earth? That I stand on the brink of dominating this planet?>

Crayak's red eye gleamed dangerously. "I am aware of everything. I am aware that in an instant I could vaporize you and this insignificant rock called Earth that you have fought so hard to conquer."

Visser One is no fool. At least, when it comes to saving his own precious hide. He bowed his head slightly.

<Of course, Crayak. I apologize for my arrogance.>

"Better," Crayak boomed. "Now . . . let's get down to business. Visser One, I desire to test the strength of my new creation. You will fight. To the death. If you win, Visser, Earth belongs to you. If my creature wins, you and your band of slugs will leave this planet. Immediately."

I grinned. Metal teeth flashed. A fight to the death!

Yes!

Again, Visser One bowed his head.

<With all due respect, Crayak, I . . . >

"You have no choice," Crayak interrupted. "So you might as well agree."

Suddenly, Crayak was in the balcony again with the Drode at its side, looking down at the arena.

"Let the games begin!" the Drode declared.

Visser One stared up at me with all four eyes.

Me, this brutal giant of an opponent.

As if hoping I might have something to say. Some explanation that would make what was happening in this dank, underground arena seem less insane.

Less bizarre.

My only response was to smile at him. Give him a look at the rows of sharklike metal teeth in my mouth.

"There," Crayak said to me. "At last you have it your way. Fight your own fight. It's all up to you, finally. No one can tell you to retreat or to surrender. There are no rules except your own."

No rules except my own!

I felt the blood rush through my powerful limbs.

. . . *the adrenaline rush of murderous desire* . . .

Felt my head expand. Imagined neurons firing.

Heard the thunderous beating of my own brave heart.

. . . reach out and destroy . . .

No rules except my own . . .

CHAPTER 20

Visser One began to circle. His wicked tail curled over his back, the blade ready to strike.

I was focused. Careful not to be sloppy, underestimate the enemy.

But I was also elated.

If I won — and there was a very, very good chance I would — Crayak would force the Yeerks out of planet Earth.

The war would be over.

No more weird alien attacks.

No more unexplained disappearances.

And everyone would know who had been responsible.

Me. Rachel.

I wouldn't overhear any more "Rachel the Wacko" remarks.

I wouldn't have to endure any more of Jake's patronizing lectures about the need for restraint. About the dark part of me that frightened everybody so badly.

No one could write me off as just another punk bully with a taste for violence.

Finally, people would see that all I'd ever wanted to do was save the planet.

To do this thing right and get it over with.

FWAP!

Visser One's tail caught me in the knees and knocked me to the ground!

Idiot! I'd been so busy dreaming about my big victory, I'd zoned out.

His tail! Coming toward my throat, preparing to slash.

I rolled out of the way.

Amazing. I disappeared in a blur!

Visser One's stalk eyes swiveled, desperately trying to locate me.

I rolled around him, a tumbling blur. Then came to a dead halt.

Jumped to my feet. Reached toward him, in-human claws extended!

He dove out of the way! Immediately started to morph.

I lurched forward and gathered his lump of a body in my massive arms. Prepared to hurl him into the back of the bleachers!

"AAAAAAHHHHH!"

I dropped the lump! My arms and chest burned as if they had been slathered with acid.

Because, in fact, they had been slathered with acid.

Visser One completed his morph. It wasn't one I recognized, but it was monstrous.

He was fifteen, twenty feet tall. Almost as tall as me!

His arms and hands dragged the ground like a gorilla's.

His skin looked reptilian, weeping and seeping some kind of acid poison.

My jaw racheted open and the sound that came out was so loud it shook the walls.

The pain was unreal. Acid penetrating, eating my flesh!

But by the time the scream was over, the pain had already gone.

My skin had morphed to meet the immediate need!

I was covered with thick, scaly plates like an alligator.

Alligator!

The moment the image flashed into my mind, I felt my snout stretch out, out, out.

A split second later I fell forward to the ground. Landed on short, sturdy alligator legs.

Instantaneous morph! In less than a second.

This was unbelievable!

I shot forward and closed my alligator jaws around the visser's leg.

CRUNCH!

I felt bones snap. The acid from his skin washed down my throat, but it barely tickled. A little hot sauce on a big, fat french fry. That was it. Just a little pleasant flavoring.

Then . . . no!

Suddenly my teeth lost their grip!

Visser One was morphing again. This time, to something gelatinous.

His melting, liquidating body seeped out of my mouth. Whatever he had become pooled on the floor in a mass of red, quivering goo.

I morphed to Super-Rachel. Stared down at the goo.

Now what?

How do you fight to the death with a puddle?

Tentatively, I stepped forward and touched it with my toe. The red goo sprang to life, like some kind of hyper-speed sludge.

My scream reverberated through the dungeon.

Then I gagged. Because the red goo was streaming into my mouth, my ears, my nose!

I raked at my face! Tore globs of goo away from my cheeks. Flung it from my fingers.

But it was no use.

It kept coming. Pouring up my body, reverse gravity, then sliding back down, then pouring back up. A vicious cycle!

I was in the grip of a gelatinous goo monster. Some hideous living sludge determined to drown me.

It didn't matter how tall I became. Or how fierce.

I couldn't fight this!

It covered me!

I was going to lose.

It was unbelievable.

I was going to lose to killer Jell-O.

CHAPTER 21

I could hear them laughing.

The Drode.

Crayak.

And David.

It was intolerable.

I had to morph. But what? What?

What had no mouth? No nose? No ears?

What could defend itself from this endless stream of runny, deadly mess?

What morphs did I have?

Birds. Fish. Mammals.

Nothing that would do me any good!

I needed to be a plant. No orifices. Something huge and hungry and dangerous.

Suddenly, I felt myself melting. Like the Wicked Witch in *The Wizard of Oz.*

Or maybe — withering. Like a tree starved for water.

Was I dying? Was this what death felt like?

My fingers lost their sensation. Human sensory ability — just gone.

Instead, they grew rubbery and ultraflexible. Not numb but — impervious to pain, to pleasure.

My lungs ceased to burn for air.

My legs! They were fusing. Braiding together at the hip. Where my feet had been, stretching out like tentacles!

Or like vines or branches . . .

Suddenly, I realized what was happening.

I wasn't dying.

I was being born.

I was becoming a living being that didn't even exist on this planet!

That I'd only imagined!

That I'd conjured into being with the force of my will!

I was morphing into something my DNA bank had absolutely nothing to do with.

A killer, carnivorous plantlike thing of my very own creation.

The red goo was no threat now. It couldn't choke or strangle me. I felt no need for air.

But I did feel hunger. And the goo looked delicious.

I bent my head, now a huge, green, veiny pod. It opened up like a flower unfolding, and a long proboscis shot out. Like the sucking organ of a giant butterfly.

I dipped it into the goo and began to drink.

The goo pulled away, startled and frightened. Began to slide across the room.

I chased it! Determined to eat it.

I approached on my magically gliding, trunk-like stem.

Thrust forward my pod-like head.

Close! Almost!

And then the goo began to morph. And in what seemed like only seconds, I found myself facing Visser One's stolen Andalite form again.

Too late to pull back!

He arched his tail. Swung his tail blade toward my vein-ribbed vegetable neck.

WHAP!

I felt my head snap off and fall to the floor.

Visser One began to laugh. And then abruptly stopped.

A tingling in my neck!

And within seconds, a second pod-like head appeared!

The visser roared angrily. No words, just a bellow of rage.

I pictured myself as Super-Rachel.

Twenty feet tall. Arms like cranes. Teeth like bear traps.

Immediately, I was as I had imagined myself.

Visser One galloped to the other side of the arena, out of my immediate reach.

I couldn't help but throw back my head. Couldn't help but laugh. Then I began to walk toward the visser. Each step a boom of thunder. The crash of a collapsing building. The smash of colliding cars.

This time, the visser didn't even try to morph. He knew it was useless. Knew the battle was over.

<This is not a fair competition!> he shouted up to Crayak. <This creature cannot be defeated.>

I flexed my hands. Saw the Drode nod and smile. I extended my cruel, steel claws. And prepared to put an end to one of the most wicked villains on this or any other planet.

<Crayak! Surely you see that this is unjust.>

I felt good to hear Visser One beg. To see him cringe.

Crayak's red eye glowed more brightly. Approvingly.

<You can't mean for me to die like this!> the visser cried.

I reached down and put my hand — it took only one — around the visser's Andalite neck.

"Finish it," Crayak said quietly.

It was unbelievable.

After all this time, I finally had him. Totally at my mercy.

With a simple squeeze I could put an end to Visser One, to the Yeerks, to this whole sorry episode of Earth's history.

All I had to do was execute him.

I'd never known true euphoria until now. What couldn't I do? There was no species in any universe that could defeat me.

I was indestructible!

I would exterminate the Yeerks. I would bring universal peace to the planet.

And then . . . and then . . .

<Spare me!> the visser pleaded.

I opened my hand. Then closed it again around his neck. Toyed with him.

<Spare me, Crayak! I will carry out your orders. Give me the powers you have given this creature and I will do your bidding, whatever it is.>

He would, too. Visser One would do anything to be endowed with the power I had now.

He would kill. He would destroy.

He would obey.

I began to squeeze. The visser's eyes — all four of them — began to bulge.

"Finish it." Crayak. "Hurry."

<Mercy,> Visser One pleaded, gasping for breath. His hooves skittered on the floor. His tail twitched helplessly. <Please!>

Visser One would obey. Just like David. Just like David's punks.

The red eye shone angrily.

"Finish it!" Crayak thundered. "What are you waiting for? Finish it or I will change you to a rat again and you will lose everything! Do you hear me? Everything!"

I tightened my grip around Visser One's neck. *Crayak could use you, Rachel.*

And I was prepared to do what Crayak asked.

CHAPTER 22

"Yes," Crayak said. "Execute him. Free the earth from tyranny. And then . . ."

And then . . . what?

Sit around and watch TV?

An ephiphany. A revelation. The lightbulb switching on in my head.

Face it, Rachel. The power is like a drug. And you are like an addict.

Would I ever get enough? How long before I turned into a morally decrepit monster like Visser One?

And making a deal with Crayak would only accelerate the journey to that inevitable end.

Suddenly, I had a vision of myself as I would

really appear to the world. To my family. Friends. To the other Animorphs. To the Chee. The free Hork-Bajir.

To every decent person on this planet.

Super-Rachel was not beautiful and kind and benevolent.

She would not be honored and respected.

She was hideous and violent and brutal.

She would be feared by everyone.

Despised and hated.

A tyrant to be plotted against, just like Visser One.

Rachel of the darkness down deep inside.

"No."

I released my grasp of Visser One's neck. Fell back, horrified at what I was about to do.

The visser dropped to the ground. Gulped air. Too stunned and frightened to move. He lay on the damp floor, his eyes following my every breath.

"What are you doing?!" Crayak thundered.

"I'm one of the good guys," I said, panting.

To my own ears, my voice sounded like a booming, grating echo. It was the voice of a doomsday machine.

"You are a fool!" Crayak shouted. "You are a coward. You are weak, sentimental, childish. Worst of all, you have wasted my time. I have tried to help you free yourself from useless human emotions, but you choose captivity instead."

WHOOSH!

Instantly, reality was altered.

Visser One was gone.

The arena or stadium was gone.

And once again, I was one of two rats in a cube.

David laughed.

"I knew it. I knew it! This is *beautiful*."

Crayak's big red eye glared at me from the other side of the clear wall.

"I offered you everything because you had the potential to win. To lead. To rule."

"That's a lie," I argued. "You just wanted to use me to kill Jake."

"Do you think the Ellimist would allow that?" Crayak hissed. "Don't you see? We are trying to bring this occupation to an end. And only a strong leader can do that."

<You could give Jake the power to end the war. If you wanted to. But you don't. Because Jake really is a strong leader, and you know it. You know you can't make him follow your rules. You know you can't control him. Well, here's some news, Crayak. You can't control me, either.>

"You'll go mad," Crayak threatened. "You'll live out your life as a rat, and you'll go mad."

I am not some kind of nut!

Who was I kidding?

The rat panicked. I panicked. Began, uncontrollably, to run around the walls of the cube. Around and around. The rat couldn't stop. I couldn't stop!

I worry about you, Rachel.

I backed off. Slipped away, deep down under the rat brain. Let it rule. Because I didn't trust my own brain.

I was afraid that I was already crazy.

Was this real?

Was it a dream?

Was it manipulated reality?

"I am real. David is real. You are real," Crayak's voice intoned.

<Stop reading my mind!>

"Time is real," it droned on. "And Cassie is real. And David and his pathetic punks are real."

<Stop! Stop!>

"And this trap is real. And you really are going to be a rat. For real. And forever."

I stopped, bumped into a corner. Collapsed onto my belly.

The light from Crayak's massive red eye again illuminated the whole ghastly scene.

Cassie in her cube, trapped, slumped over. Looking across at me in despair.

The two punks, cowering in a corner of the

dungeon. Definitely freaked out beyond descrip-
tion. Trying, futilely, to hide from the searching
red glow.

David. In a furry, red-tinged lump not two feet
from me.

Slowly, the red light began to fade.

Going.

Going.

Until it was gone altogether.

Suddenly, I was cold. It was a shock. Like the
temperature had plunged from ninety to thirty
degrees in a matter of seconds.

Whatever energy Crayak's presence had cre-
ated had disappeared along with it. Once again,
the dungeon was sunk into a dark, damp gloom.

Crayak and the Drode were gone.

They had disappeared back into the vastness
of the universe. Maybe forever.

And I was on my own.

With only minutes until I was trapped in rat
morph. Definitely forever.

CHAPTER 23

No help was coming. That much I knew. Nobody knew where I had gone. Not my family. Not Jake and the others. How could they?

If anybody was going to save me and save Cassie, it was going to have to be me.

Not Super-Rachel. Not enhanced Rachel. Not even human-Rachel.

The only Rachel around was rat-Rachel.

I had no power. No weapons. No room to morph anything of significance.

Nothing!

David was loving my defeat. Gloating.

<You blew it! You had your chance and you blew it big time. Crayak's through with you. You failed. You bored it. Now it's out of here. Gone!>

I worry about you, Rachel.

<Now it's just us, Rachel. Just you and me. Rachel and David. But don't worry. We'll be just fine. I'll show you how to get by. I've still got a couple of henchmen. Right now they're pee-in-their-pants scared, but they'll do for the moment. In fact, Rachel, if we play our cards right and work real hard, we should be able to put together a big enough payroll to hire more muscle. A few guys less wimpy than those two pathetic losers in the corner.>

I am not some kind of nut.

And right then, a light went on in my little rat brain.

Another revelation, epiphany, realization.

Like David said, Tattoo and Grease were still crouched in the corner. No doubt trying to figure out if it was safe to step out of the shadows.

<Hey! You with the tattoo.>

He turned, startled.

<Yeah, you. How much is he paying you?> I asked.

<Don't answer that,> David ordered.

Tattoo and Grease looked nervously at each other.

"Let's get out of here," Grease whispered. Loudly.

Tattoo nodded.

<How much did he say he had stashed

131

away?> I said. Loudly. <Two hundred and twelve thousand dollars? That's a hundred and six thousand dollars for each of you.>

Bingo. I had their attention now.

First Tattoo then Grease got to his feet. Came over to the cube, slowly. Looked down at me with interest.

<Nice try, Rachel,> David sneered. <There's only one problem. The money is where no one but I can find it! I've got you, Rachel. I've got you. One minute to go and you're my rat queen!>

That was so not going to happen.

<You guys like working down here in the sewer?> I asked Grease. My tone demanding, strong. <You like taking orders from a talking rat? Wouldn't you rather have the money? All the money? Now, instead of later? Imagine what you could do with a hundred and six thousand dollars each.>

<Shut up!> David cried. <Shut up. They're not very smart. You'll just confuse them. And when they get confused they get meaner and stupider than they already are!>

Grease took a gun from inside his jacket and banged the barrel against the glass.

"You shut up," he said to David. Then to me, "He's right. We don't know where the money is, and we can't find it."

Elation! It was more satisfying than any power high. I was on my way out of this trap. And, funny. I hadn't had to use force, or terror, or pain.

Just my brains.

<You're right,> I told them.

I glanced at the clock.

Thirty seconds.

Twenty-nine seconds.

<No human would be able to find David's stash. But another rat? Another rat could find it easy. Like me. I could follow his scent. I could track back wherever he's been.>

<What do you want?> Grease demanded.

Not so dumb after all.

<I want you to let me out of this box. Just for a second. Okay? So I don't get trapped as a rat forever. Then I'll morph back to rat and get the money for you.>

Eighteen seconds.

Seventeen seconds.

"How do we know you'll come back?" Tattoo asked.

It was all I could do not to scream. I forced myself to stay calm. To speak slowly. To sound sincere.

<You'll still have Cassie as a hostage.>

<It's a trap,> David squeaked. <A trap, you idiots! Don't fall for it.>

133

Tattoo and Grease eyed David with contempt.

Sometimes it pays to have a dark heart. It helps you to understand other dark hearts.

I knew exactly what the two punks were thinking. They wanted the money because, to them, money was power. It was freedom from having to take orders from David, someone they disliked and feared.

Tattoo and Grease wanted to be in charge.

Didn't we all?

Five seconds.

Four seconds.

<You've got one second or the deal's off the table,> I said.

Tattoo pointed his gun at the lock on the box and fired.

BANG!

Two seconds.

I leaped! There were no steel coils in my joints, but the rat's legs were powerful enough. I was demorphing before my nose even touched the lid of the box.

Boing!

The lid sprang open. I heard David squeak in protest as some part of my partly formed human body — probably a foot — crowded him into a corner.

My legs stretched out. Little claws expanded, extended into toes.

Suddenly — I couldn't breathe! The elongated rat snout retracted into my skull and filled my sinus cavity.

Swoosh!

Yes. Human nose!

A tickling pain at the base of my spine.

Then — Pop!

The rat tail reconfigured itself into a human spinal column.

My eyes were changing, vision shifting madly. But I kept a passing image of the clock.

Click!

No!

The counter turned to zero.

I was in midmorph.

Was I going to make it all the way out?

My arms were tiny. Not yet grown. Where fingers should be, there were still little fur-covered paws.

I looked down. My thighs, still curved into huge haunches.

I was a rat girl.

Trapped in midmorph!

I heard David laugh.

"Oh, my God! You're hideous. This is even better than I'd hoped!"

I closed my eyes. I would not let this happen. I refused to let it happen!

I summoned every ounce of morphing energy.

Every ounce of mental energy. Every ounce of concentration.

I blotted out every random thought. Tried desperately to dampen every wild emotion.

But there was something in the way. Something stubborn and intractable that would not be ignored.

It was the hate. The anger.

I tried! I tried to push it away!

But the truth was I didn't want it to go away. I wanted my anger. I wanted my hate.

It was the source of my strength.

And then . . . miraculously . . . I stood and spread my arms wide.

I was Rachel.

I was back.

And for the moment, I really was free.

CHAPTER 24

I opened my eyes.

Tattoo and Grease were staring at me, mouths open.

It was hard to believe that anything could really surprise them at this point.

Not after Crayak. The Drode. Magically appearing aliens with blue fur and four eyes.

Grease recovered first. He lifted his gun and pointed it at me.

"Okay, kid. It's back to rat now. Time to show us the money."

I nodded.

"Sure. But if it's okay with you, I'm going to morph something with an even better sense of smell. I'll be able to find the money faster."

I started the morph before they could give permission or ask questions.

I felt the old familiar snap, crackle, and pop as my face ripped open. Muzzle extended. Shoulders bulked.

"Hey!" I heard one punk cry. Tattoo. "What's she doing?"

"Probably something big and scary so she can hold up a bank," Grease said solemnly.

Yeah. Right. In his imbecilic dreams.

Within seconds, the morph was complete.

I stood up on my hind legs and started toward them.

"What's she doing?" Grease yelled, backing up, shakily pointing his gun at me.

<She's getting ready to eat you for lunch, you stupid idiot!> David screamed. He jumped out of the cube. Scampered down the leg of the table. And he ran.

My weak grizzly eyes saw him disappear into the shadows.

"Hey! Where are you going?" Grease yelled after him.

I lunged with all the speed and bulk of the grizzly.

Man! I love that morph.

Tattoo and Grease fought me. They slapped and kicked. Like swatting mosquitoes. Total piece of cake. So easy, it wasn't even fun.

Yeah, they fired their guns. But the shots went way wide.

Panic will screw up your aim every time.

I rolled over them. Literally. Threw myself at them and rolled.

Somersaulted.

Knocked the guns out of their hands.

Then I let them get to their feet. Which by this point wasn't very easy for them to do.

When they were up I roared.

That was all it took.

Tattoo and Grease ran, squealing like stuck pigs. Scrambled up the side of the far wall. Used broken stones and bricks as handholds and toeholds.

They were headed for the manhole cover. Through which they would escape into the world above.

Where they would talk. Incoherently, in a bar somewhere, maybe on a street corner.

Most people wouldn't believe a word of the punks' story.

But eventually, a Controller would hear and believe.

And the Yeerks would know that somewhere there was a rat who knew all about the Animorphs.

Something would have to be done.

There was no sound effect. No WHOOSH! But

139

I felt all the optimism and elation rush out of the atmosphere. Felt my stomach plummet.

Something would have to be done. And I would have to do it.

Wasn't this how the whole thing had started?

I ran over to the cube in which Cassie was held prisoner. Dug my claws into the lock. It popped easily, and I opened the top.

Cassie climbed out, her face damp with perspiration.

"Rachel! Morph and let's get out of here," she said quickly. "As soon as those two start talking, somebody will be down here to investigate. We need to be far away."

I nodded. <I know. But you go. I'll catch up.>

Cassie put her hand on my massive arm. "What are you going to do?"

I looked into Cassie's eyes. Did she want to know? Did she really want to know?

No. She didn't.

That's why I'd been so angry. Not just at Jake. At all of them.

Because they had kept their hands clean. They had pretended they didn't know I'd done something extreme like threaten to kill David. And his parents.

And when David had confronted them with the truth, they'd made their disapproval known. Separated themselves from me. Made it clear I was deranged and out of control and so, so unlike them.

And then, Cassie had come up with the plan to trap David in morph. But only I'd had the nerve to endure the two gut-wrenching hours of David's misery.

Why hadn't I fought back? Defended myself against accusations, insinuations of craziness?

Okay, I'd confronted Jake. But had anything really changed between us since then?

Did he generally approve of my actions? No. Only of their results. He needed my results.

So why had I been carrying around all that guilt, all by myself? Why had I been shouldering so much of the pain?

I looked at Cassie's face. It was a sweet face. It was wise, too. But still . . . I don't know . . . oddly innocent somehow.

I'd been protecting her. Them.

Jake. Cassie. Tobias. Even Marco and Ax. Helping to protect their innocence. Letting them see themselves as the good guys.

It was a symbiotic relationship. Or co-dependent, whatever.

They needed me to be the bad guy.

And I needed them to be the good guys.

See, if they were the good guys, and I was on their team, then that automatically made me a good guy, too. Even if I was different.

141

At least that's what I'd been telling myself.

Of course, it wasn't quite that simple.

"Rachel! What are you going to do?" Cassie pressed.

<I'm going after David.>

She shook her head. "Don't. Let him go."

"He'll go to the Yeerks," I said. "Or the Yeerks will come to him. Either way, he'll tell them everything. He'll betray us, hoping to make a deal. It won't work. The Yeerks will kill him. Then they'll find us. So I'm going to find David, first. And I'm going to take him back to the island."

"I don't think you can do it a second time," Cassie said quietly.

I felt all the old anger bubbling up. Why was she arguing? She knew what had to be done. Why was she pretending not to understand what had to be done?

So she could sleep at night? So she could say "I tried to stop her, so it's not my fault?" So she could say "I didn't know."

I looked her in the eye.

<I'm not sure I can, either. So will you do it?>

Cassie's face creased. Her mouth opened and closed. Her eyes flickered.

"I don't know," she whispered finally.

<I didn't think so.>

CHAPTER 25

If I got out of this one alive, I was never going to use my rat morph again. Ever.

I sniffed around the dungeon until I picked up David's scent. He'd gone deeper into the sewer. I followed the spore into a narrow pipe.

The pipe was rusted inside. The rust gave my claws some traction. Little feet scrabbling along — the sound that pursued the guilty and grossed out the innocent and made them shudder.

I thought for a moment about how horribly close I had come to being trapped forever as a rat. The thought made me ill.

It would be devastating. To watch people recoil at the very sight of me.

Awful to live in the shadows.

Hideous to be in constant fear of being killed or eaten. Or of starving to death, slowly, painfully.

How had David done it?

How had he survived?

I pushed the thought away. I'd been down that road too many times. And I knew on that road lay madness.

I stopped for a moment. Listened. Far above me, I heard another set of claws.

David.

We'd have to get out of the pipe. I couldn't beat him in rat morph. I'd have to be able to morph human or maybe cat to overcome him. Something bigger and stronger.

Sudden silence.

The scampering feet came to a stop.

Had David exited the pipe?

I sniffed and doubled my speed. Up the pipe. Down the pipe. Around a bend. Around another bend.

Finally, something bright up ahead.

Sunlight.

Suddenly I realized how much I needed air and light. How much I had been craving a release from the stifling darkness.

I shot out of the sewer pipe.

And saw him.

David.

He was sitting on his haunches, looking up at the sun. His tiny paws waved gracefully in the air, helping him keep his balance. His pink nose sniffed appreciatively. His delicate whiskers waved slightly in the breeze.

He knew I was there.

<It's a beautiful world,> he said thickly. <I'll miss it.>

I waited for him to run. To try to escape. But he didn't.

I looked around. Were his henchmen waiting? Had he lured me into a trap?

<There's no one here but us,> he said. <The punks are gone.>

<Then what's going on?>

David dropped down on all fours and faced me.

<It's over. You won.>

I began to demorph. When I was human again, I squatted and David approached me. Sat at my feet.

<Without Crayak, without help, I can't beat you, Rachel. And I'm tired of trying. But I won't go back,> he said forcefully. <I'd rather die than go back to that island. You'll have to kill me.>

"I won't do that," I said.

He tried to run. I reached out and grabbed him. Easily.

<Kill me,> David begged. <I'd rather die than

145

go on like this. Rather die than go back to that place!>

"You're going back to the island."

David struggled in my hand. I tightened my grip.

<I won't go back,> he cried. <Kill me, Rachel! If there's any humanity left in you at all, please kill me.>

"I'm one of the good guys," I choked. Tears welled up in my eyes.

<Then do the good thing!>

David struggled even harder. I held on tight. I knew I was hurting him. But if I let him go . . .

"Promise to disappear," I said suddenly. "Promise to disappear and . . ."

David began to laugh through his sobs.

<Crayak was right. You are a fool. I can't go back to what I was. You know that!>

I lifted David and looked into his tiny dark eyes. Something wet fell on his head.

My tears. I tried to brush them away, but they kept coming. I didn't want to kill him. I didn't want to take him back to the island.

In spite of everything, I felt sorry for him.

I felt sorry for David and sorry for me. Sorry for what the war had done to us both.

It wasn't David's fault that he was a rat, that he was insane. He was what we had made him.

But that didn't make him any less dangerous.

We couldn't control him. We couldn't trust him. And on the loose, he could destroy the entire planet.

Maybe.

"I don't know what to do," I whispered, my throat working.

<I can't help you, Rachel.>

I put him down on the dirty pavement, gently. Then I put my head on my arms and I cried.

It's all up to you . . . . There are no rules except your own.

Maybe he would run away. Maybe he would disappear into a baseboard somewhere where I could never find him.

You have free will. What you do with it is up to you.

Maybe when I lifted my head he wouldn't be there.

And he wouldn't be my problem anymore.

Let Cassie find him and do something. Or Jake. Or Marco. Or Ax. Somebody — *anybody* — but me!

It's all up to you, Rachel.

I cried like a baby.

It wasn't the first time since the war started.

So many losses. So much pain.

I hoped to hear the sound of little rat feet scurrying away.

Please go, I thought. *Please. Run. Run away from me!*

147

But when I finally lifted my head, I saw David through the blur of my tears. Sitting patiently. Waiting.

He wasn't going to go away.

He wasn't going to make it easy.

<Just kill me,> he said softly.

I wiped my sleeve across my face.

"I'm one of the good guys," I muttered. At that moment I felt more exhausted than I ever had in my entire life.

<Then do the right thing.>

I looked around. Stupidly. There was no one to tell me what to do.

No Crayak. No Ellimist.

No Cassie. No Jake.

I was alone with David.

My enemy was completely at my mercy.

I caught a glimpse of myself in a broken shard of mirror.

And saw what anyone looking down the alleyway from the sidewalk would have seen.

A young girl sitting knees-up in the sun, staring at a white rat.

It would be hard to believe the entire fate of the planet depended on that girl.

A girl who wanted to do the right thing.

But who had no idea at all what that was. . . .

Don't miss

#49 The Diversion

"Let me get this straight." Marco shredded a piece of hay. "They wanted blood samples. Not cash. Not drugs. Blood."

We were in Cassie's barn. The Wildlife Rehabilitation Clinic. Sort of a homeless shelter for wounded animals. Cassie's parents were both veterinarians. Her mom worked at The Gardens, a combination zoo/amusement park where we'd acquired most of our battle morphs. Her dad ran the clinic here on their farm. Cassie helped him out.

At the moment she was inside a big wire pen, doctoring a doe that had been shot in the thigh. The rest of us were trying not to focus on the hypodermic needle in her hand.

"The rest of us" could've starred in one of those weepy movies on Lifetime. Jake: Rachel's cousin, Cassie's true love, and the leader of our little band of misfits. Ax the alien: Elfangor's little brother and, strange as it sounds, my uncle. Marco: Jake's best friend and Ax's part-time roommate. Rachel, of course: Cassie's best friend, the girl dating out of her species. And me: Tobias. Bird-boy. On lookout duty in the rafters.

Cassie stroked the deer's neck. "It's okay, girl."

Ax reached into the pen and stroked the animal. He was in his natural Andalite form. It wouldn't have surprised me if the doe viewed him as a distant cousin. An eccentric distant cousin who ate through his hooves.

Cassie closed the pen and turned to face us. "All I know is what my mom said. Two men broke into her veterinary ward last night. It wasn't the usual smash and grab, and no, they weren't after drugs, which surprised Mom, too. They wanted blood samples, specific blood samples. Tiger. Elephant. Eagle. Rhino and grizzly. Gorilla and wolf."

Rachel stared at her. "Our battle morphs."

"Right." Cassie nodded. "They showed no interest in the warthogs or baboons. One of Mom's lab techs stumbled in on them. They really roughed him up, especially —" She glanced at me. "Especially when he told them The Gardens didn't have a red-tailed hawk."

Seven pairs of eyes, including Ax's stalk eyes, gazed up at the rafters. I turned away to preen a wing.

Cassie went on. "The lab tech said they'd been cold and methodical up to that point, but when they couldn't get the hawk sample, they just went nuts. Like they were afraid to leave without it."

"Yeah, I bet," said Marco. "I bet they were peeing their pants wondering how to explain the concept of failure to Visser One."

Visser One. Evil incarnate. The Yeerk in charge of the invasion of Earth, recently promoted from Visser Three.

Elfangor's murderer. Actually, he was responsible for a lot more deaths than we even knew about.

Rachel nodded. "Our battle morphs? The Gardens? Nutso thieves on a mission for hawk blood? Definitely Yeerks."

"Uh, yeah," Jake agreed. "But the Chee haven't heard anything, not even rumors. And we haven't intercepted Yeerk communications about a new project. Whatever they're up to, it's at the highest level. We don't want to do anything stupid. We need to really think this through."

"Okay, so we'll think it through and then we'll do something stupid," said Marco. "First question: Why do the Yeerks need animal blood? Have they invented a new way to morph?"

<Invented?> Ax's stalk eyes narrowed to slits. <Yeerks do not invent. They steal. Everything

they have, they've taken from other species. Most notably the Andalites. They do not have the intelligence — or the integrity — to invent a morphing technique of their own.>

Did I mention Andalites can be a wee bit arrogant?

Cassie looked at Jake.

"I think Ax is right," he said. "They're after something bigger. Tom brought home a flyer yesterday. The Sharing is sponsoring a hugh blood drive."

Tom was Jake's older brother.

Tom was a Controller, a high-ranking member of The Sharing. The front organization for the Yeerks.

Cassie took a deep breath. "Here's what I think. There's only one reason the Yeerks would suddenly be interested in blood. DNA. They're collecting samples of our morph animals, and they're collecting as many human samples as they can." She looked at us. "They're searching for humans with strands of animal DNA in their blood."

Silence.

"Which means —" Marco sighed.

"They know we're human," said Rachel.

The Secret Is No More

ANIMORPHS

K. A. Applegate

Everything the Animorphs have ever known is about to change. The Yeerks suspect that the Andalite bandits are human after all. It's only a matter of time before the Animorphs are found and infested or killed. Something drastic has to happen. Because now, the Animorphs may have to tell you who they are—and that changes everything.

ANIMORPHS #49: THE DIVERSION

Coming to Bookstores this December

Visit the Web site at: www.scholastic.com/animorphs

Watch for the GTI game in September 2000

ANIT1200